FILTHY WOLF

JUNKYARD SHIFTERS, BOOK 2

LIZA STREET

Filthy Wolf, Junkyard Shifters, Book 2

by Liza Street

Cover designed by Keira Blackwood.

1

The small room, stuffed with twenty people and a monster, was unnaturally quiet.

Jessica narrowed her gaze at the monster in question. Professor Chaole (pronounced *kale*, which seemed apt to Jessica, who hated kale) was a slender woman with a huge head of blond hair. She wore her hair in a loose bun that flopped this way and that as she moved. Slenderness and blondness weren't particularly monstrous attributes. No, it was the vitriol and venom that spewed from Chaole's mouth when she critiqued student manuscripts.

If it weren't for Chaole, the room, with cheerful sunlight streaming through the windows, would probably make everyone pleasantly tired. Instead, every single person was on edge, even Chaole's favorite writing students.

The current student in the hot seat, Gregory, was holding his notebook in front of him. He'd paused during his reading to take in Chaole's stern expression. Not reassured in the slightest, he continued his chapter in a shaky voice. "And she was held fast, treasured, in the jaws of the beast."

As Gregory lowered his notebook, Chaole sighed. "Derivative. Prosaic. The premise relies on clichés and tropes. Where is the magic in this piece? Where is the *literature*? It is all so mundane. It makes me want to shoot myself in the fucking head."

Two weeks ago, when this intensive writing retreat began, words like those might have caused some of the students to gasp. Now, however, they knew better.

Gregory nodded and returned to his seat.

"That concludes our disappointing critique session this afternoon," Chaole said. "Remember, absolute silence must be adhered to until dinner at six."

Jessica sighed inwardly, picked up her notebook, and started for the door. The rules here were intense. No phones. No talking except at lunch and dinner. No computers. All writing would be done by hand.

Two or three of the hopeful authors seemed to be thriving with these restrictions in place. If Jessica had to hear one more time about Leah's "award-winning draft," Jessica just might throw up.

Jessica didn't belong here. Unfortunately, her parents had sent her here as a last-ditch effort to develop her writing skills.

She was a college graduate, dammit. She should have the nerve to tell her parents she didn't want to follow in their footsteps.

And yet here she was, stuck in the middle of nowhere in an intensive writing program run by Machiavelli's long-lost sister.

"Blythe," Chaole said. "A word, please."

Jessica purposefully dropped her pen and bent behind a row of folding metal chairs to pick it up. Blythe, a stunning redhead, was one of the few students who had tried befriending Jessica *without* knowing who Jessica's parents were. It had instantly endeared Jessica to her, and they usually sat together at lunch and dinner.

However, Chaole seemed to have it out for Blythe. Jessica was determined to figure out why.

"Hello, Professor Chaole," Blythe said quietly.

"The pages you turned in last night are absolute crap, do you know that?" Chaole asked.

Blythe's voice was soft, yet there was a thread of confidence in it. "I believed they were a decent start for my first chapter."

"I threw them in the recycling. Start over."

"But Professor Chaole—"

"Don't insult my intelligence with such dross, Blythe. I don't know how you got into this program, but if you don't improve, you'll be going home early."

"I understand."

Jessica hated the way Blythe's voice wavered.

A chapter. Chaole had *thrown away* a student's writing? And when they were writing out their chapters on paper, that meant it wasn't backed up on a computer somewhere.

That was just wrong.

Blythe hurried out of the building, her curly, orange-red hair swishing behind her. Jessica scampered after her along the worn dirt path through the trees. Probably alerted by Jessica's footsteps, Blythe turned. She smiled weakly at Jessica.

"That's messed up," Jessica whispered as quietly as possible.

Blythe shrugged. "It's what we're here for, I guess."

"Do you want me to help you fish them out of the recycling bin? We can go tonight after lights out."

"Sweet of you to offer," Blythe whispered, her smile

growing bigger, "but I started copying my chapters down in another notebook on day two, after Chaole tore Amanda's in half."

She pointed to the messenger bag slung over her shoulder.

"That's smart," Jessica said, giving Blythe a high-five.

Jessica was about to turn away when she noticed Blythe's eyes shining with unshed tears. They passed two student cabins and reached Blythe's.

"I don't understand why she's so mean to you," Jessica said.

"Probably because I'm a charity case. I mean, scholarship student." Blythe shrugged.

Immediately feeling guilty for her own wealth, Jessica looked down. She didn't even want to be here, whereas students in Blythe's situation had to apply for special grants and scholarships just to attend.

On the ground was a little flowering plant, nestled among the dry, rocky soil. It was a Plumas rayless daisy. Jessica had seen one the other day and looked it up in one of the guides in the dining hall.

She was about to point the flowers out to Blythe when Blythe said, "I wish I didn't have to go in there and face my terrible chapter."

"You don't," Jessica said, pulling her attention away from the daisies.

Blythe raised her eyebrows.

"Seriously," Jessica said. "Come to my cabin instead. It's not like Chaole comes to check on us or anything. As long as we're quiet, no one will know we're breaking rules."

From the cabin adjacent to Blythe's came a scraping noise. Jessica looked over in time to see one of the windows sliding open. Leah poked her head out and made an exaggerated *shh* motion with her finger to her lips. Jessica was tempted to make a one-finger gesture of her own. Instead, she stared hard at Leah until Leah pulled her head back into her cabin and closed the window.

"So?" Jessica said, raising her eyebrows.

"I don't know," Blythe said.

"I have tequila," Jessica said.

Blythe's face broke in silent laughter. "Lead the way."

They hurried to Jessica's cabin, which was luckily at the end of the row. Amanda wrote with music, wearing headphones, so Jessica knew they wouldn't disturb her even if they got giggly. Jessica was so ready to let loose. It felt irresponsible, sure, but after two weeks of being treated like a rebellious teenager, maybe it was time to act like one.

After two shots each, they were comparing notes on the first stories they'd written. Each of them had been preteens when they started. Jessica, at the urging of her parents. Blythe, at the urging of a supportive teacher.

"It was loosely based fanfic," Blythe said. "I should've known then that I'd never cut it as a writer."

"Are you freaking kidding me?" Jessica shook her head and gave Blythe the sternest look she could manage. "I heard you read during the workshops. Your writing is so good. Don't ever let a stuffy old monster like Chaole make you think otherwise."

Blythe smiled. "She is kind of stuffy, isn't she?"

"You did see her face when Harold started reading that bedroom scene he wrote, right?"

They cackled. The scene had been truly awful, going on and on about the female character's pert breasts with their perfect little nipple buttons.

"Buttons," Blythe laughed, "like you just push them and *bam*, she's turned on."

Jessica was laughing so hard she was gasping. She poured them each a third shot. They clinked their glasses together, then drank up.

"So, like..." Blythe hesitated, fiddling with a lock of her red hair.

Jessica was pretty sure Blythe was going to ask about her parents. But she didn't mind—she wasn't getting any of the fangirl vibes from Blythe like she often got from so-called "friends" who wanted to hang out with her because her parents were famous. It was even worse with writer friends. They seemed to want to hang out with Jessica because she could get them an audience or connection to her parents.

"Go on," Jessica said.

"I don't want to be a dick and ask what it was like growing up with Carlos and Donna Valdez," Blythe said, "but...I'm dying to know because you're so chill and nice. You don't have to talk about it if you don't want, though. I'm sure you're tired of being asked."

"It's okay," Jessica said. She was just relieved Blythe hadn't asked for their email addresses or for Jessica to pass Blythe's manuscript along to them to read. That was a disappointment she'd experienced dozens of times. "They're great parents. Truly. I'm very lucky."

"It does seem that way," Blythe said. The darkness in her slate-green eyes hinted at a much different childhood.

"Yeah. If I can have one complaint, though, it's that they want me to be an author like them. They say it's 'in my blood.'"

Blythe leaned forward. "What do *you* think?"

"I think if it's in my blood, it's skipping a generation. If I have a kid someday, maybe the author gene will manifest in them."

"I think your writing is good," Blythe said.

Jessica looked at her. Blythe wasn't the type to use the word *good* if she could say something else.

"But I don't have the spark," Jessica said.

Blythe nodded, then winced. "I'm sorry. It's not—crap. I shouldn't have nodded. I'm so sorry."

"Oh my gosh, don't be," Jessica said, gratitude blooming in her chest. "It's the first honest thing anyone has told me about my writing. Everyone else just wants to be my friend because, well, my parents. So they're fake."

"I promise, I'm not being fake," Blythe said. "I'm just glad you're not pissed at me and kicking me out of your cabin."

"You didn't insult me. You validated what I've been feeling all this time. I'm grateful." Impulsively, Jessica leaned forward and hugged Blythe. Pulling away again, she said, "Now take out that so-called crap chapter and impress my socks off."

As she listened to Blythe read from her extra notebook, she couldn't believe how miserable she'd been two hours ago, listening to Chaole berate all the students during the workshop. And now she was in here with a friend, and listening to the sparkling prose of a scene that was seriously publication-ready.

And, maybe for the first time, she had a friend.

"Come on," Blythe said, "let's get some writing done."

"You'll hang out here and write with me?" Jessica asked, feeling hopeful.

Blythe nodded. "Yes. But no more drinking. We both have work to do."

Marcus caught Lena's scent in the air. She smelled like mint and copper or something metallic. He'd always liked the combination— a sharp and feminine aroma that got his heart beating faster. At least, it had done so until he learned she didn't have the same feelings. Now it just caused an ache.

Quickening his pace, he pushed those thoughts away. Despite any ache or remaining yearning, he still looked forward to seeing her on the other side of the boundary. She'd have a message from his half-sister, Marianne, and he was eager for news. And then he'd be able to talk to Lena for a little while, which was just as good as hearing from Marianne.

Which made him feel like the biggest asshole. Lena had a mate. A mate she was wildly in love with. Marcus, unfortunately, had been friend-zoned from the very beginning.

He followed her scent to the pond at the northwest boundary of the Junkyard. She stood just on the other side of the gravel line.

Unfortunately, she wasn't alone.

Another woman stood at her side. She had wild blond curls and wore bright pink lipstick. Marcus gave an experimental sniff. He detected the dusty scent of a big cat—that was Lena. He could also detect the mossy scent of a wolf shifter—so the other woman was a wolf like him.

The woman smiled at him, but when he tried to smile back, his mouth barely moved.

Lena frowned and gave him a subtle shake of her head, a wordless admonition to be nice.

Why had she brought someone else?

"Lena," he said. "Good to see you."

"You, too." She grinned. "This is Cassie. I was talking about you yesterday, and she wanted to meet you."

"Hi," Marcus said to Cassie. He held up his left hand, as he no longer had a right one. "I'd offer to shake your hand, but as you probably know, I'm stuck here."

"But I could put my hand over the line to shake yours," Cassie said.

"Yeah, but why would you do that?" Marcus asked.

"Maybe you'd yank me over the line, and I'd be stuck with you," she said, looking as if the idea wasn't at all unappealing.

Marcus gaped at her.

Lena gave her a strange look.

"Do you have a message from Marianne?" Marcus asked Lena.

"Yep." Lena pulled a piece of paper from her back pocket and handed it to Marcus. "You should let her come and visit you. She really wants to."

That was out of the question. Marianne would not be allowed to set foot anywhere near the Junkyard. Marcus shook his head. "You know how I feel about that, Lena."

"It's been almost two months. She misses you."

"She's *human*. It would be a disaster."

"I agree," Cassie said, even though no one had asked her. "What you boys need in there are some real shifter women."

Marcus didn't know what to say to that. Lena had been in here, not long ago, and it had caused a whole lot of trouble. It hadn't been Lena's fault, but still, the tragedy had been complete. Their friend Kyle died. Marcus lost his right hand. Lena and her mate, Carter, had barely made it out alive.

"Lena," Cassie said, a smile pasted on her face, "do you think I could talk to Marcus for a few minutes?"

"Sure," Lena said, although she looked less than enthusiastic, probably realizing, as Marcus did, that Cassie was not quite as well-adjusted as Lena might have originally thought. "I wanted to talk to Caitlyn, anyway."

She took off toward Caitlyn and Grant's cabin, sending an apologetic look over her shoulder to Marcus.

Yeah, she should be sorry. First she went and fell in love with Carter, and now she was bringing random women along with her when she came to visit Marcus.

Oh, shit. He suddenly realized what this was supposed to be.

Lena was *matchmaking*.

He would've laughed if it wasn't so fucking depressing.

"So, tell me something about yourself, Marcus," Cassie said.

"Well. I'm a murderer," Marcus said.

Cassie nodded. "I figured you must've done something bad to get thrown in there."

"Yep. Cold-blooded killer, that's me."

"I don't mind," Cassie said. "How many guys are in the Junkyard, anyway? I have friends. The girls and I talk about this place a lot."

"You do?"

"Yeah. We call ourselves the Junkyard Groupies."

Marcus could only stare at her.

She went on, "When we found out Lena had gone in there to find herself a mate, it got us talking."

Ho-ly shit. This was not right. Lena hadn't come in here to find a mate, and it was surely the worst possible reason for getting stuck in the Junkyard. Marcus was careful not to use the word "crazy" in situations that didn't call for it, but this woman was...well, she was crazy if she thought getting tossed in the Junkyard would land her a mate.

"Lena!" Marcus shouted. He needed to get this woman out of here. "Lena!"

Cassie took another step toward the gravel line. "I could come in there right now and find my fated mate. A bad boy who will rock my world like Carter rocks Lena's."

"That is *not* how this works," Marcus said. Cassie was way too close to the gravel line. "Lena! Get your ass back here now!"

"How do you know?" Cassie asked, looking pointedly at his right arm and the space where his hand should have been. "If you and I aren't compatible—and probably we're not, because I like my men *whole*—well, there are plenty of other guys in there, right?"

Sounds came from the trees—Lena and Grant running toward him and Cassie. Thank fuck. Imagine being trapped in here with someone like Cassie. The Junkyard was bad enough as it was.

Looking over at them, Cassie sighed. "I could do it, you know. Step right over that line."

Grant and Lena reached them and Grant said to Cassie, "My mate was tied up and would have been gravely harmed if I hadn't been able to save her. There are good guys in here, like Marcus, and there are some really, really bad ones."

"Exactly," Cassie said, smiling and taking a step forward.

Lena grabbed one of her arms, Grant grabbed the other one. Marcus was ready to block her from this side, but there was only so much he could do to keep her out.

"You need to let me go! I need to find my mate!" Cassie yelled.

Just then, Barnum came around the edge of the boulder nearest the pond. He was a giant with brown hair and eyes that didn't seem to hold any depth or any real emotion.

Marcus pointed to him. "How about this guy? You want him for a mate?"

"Fuck yeah," Barnum said, hurrying over to the boundary line. "Come in here, baby. I can take care of you."

He grabbed his crotch and leered, and Cassie's eyes bugged out. She shook her head and allowed Lena and Grant to pull her back another few steps.

"See?" Marcus said to her. He could have hugged Barnum for showing up right then.

"Come on," Grant said to Cassie. "Let's go meet Caitlyn."

Cassie and Grant walked away, and Lena faced Marcus and Barnum.

"Sorry," Lena said.

"Yeah, me too," Barnum said. "She looked like a good time."

Lena sneered. "You're disgusting."

"Get out of here, Barnum," Marcus said.

Shrugging, Barnum ambled off, muttering about assholes and bitches. Which made this just like any other Tuesday.

"What were you thinking?" Marcus said to Lena.

"I was thinking that you need someone," Lena said, folding her arms across her chest.

Un-fucking-believable. "I don't need anybody."

"But you could get out, if you found a mate," Lena said. "I mean, obviously not Cassie. But someone else. And you could've been nicer to Cassie from the start."

"Okay, first," Marcus said, "has it ever occurred to you that maybe I should stay in here? That my alpha put me in this place for a reason?"

"Yeah, but I *know* you," Lena said.

"And second, I don't want a mate. There is no one in this world for me. So thanks for thinking of me, but don't do this again."

She wore a stubborn look, and her blue eyes flashed. "Marcus Bylund, you need to get free of that attitude. No, you absolutely should *not* stay in the Junkyard, and yes, there *is* a woman out there for you."

There was no sense arguing with her; she'd never see reason. "Okay, thanks, Lena."

He turned to go.

"Marcus, don't you dare dismiss me like that and walk off."

Whirling to face her, he glared right back into her blue eyes. "What do you want me to say, Lena? I believe what I believe. I'd thought there might be someone for me, but I was wrong. So let it go."

He didn't tell her that the person he'd thought might be for him, was her.

"Fine." She put her hands at her hips. "Are you going to write back to Marianne?"

He looked down at the note from Marianne still clutched in his hand; he'd forgotten about it. "Yeah."

He'd brought a pen with him and took it from his pocket to clumsily write out a message with his left hand. He was getting better at writing left-handed, but it still wasn't pretty. That was okay, though, because Lena would type the message into an email, anyway. As long as Lena could read it to transcribe it, his handwriting was good enough.

Marianne's message wasn't long. She mostly wanted to know when she could come to visit Marcus. *Never,* Marcus thought, although the idea of never seeing his half-sister again made his chest hurt.

Things are too dangerous here, he wrote. *I'll let Lena know when you can come. I miss you too, sis.* He hadn't saved her from one monster only to have her put at risk from others. And he could imagine several different scenarios in which the Junkyard shifters tried to get her over the boundary line. He knew how resourceful some of them could be. They'd tricked Caitlyn into the territory earlier in the year.

Then again, maybe no tricking was necessary—Cassie and the Junkyard Groupies would waltz over voluntarily if given half a chance.

"Marcus," Lena said as he folded up the note. "Really. Are you okay?"

"I'm good," he said.

She wrinkled her nose, as if trying to scent a lie, but *I'm good* was true enough to pass. Happy? No. But alive and surviving? That was good.

The note passed easily through the invisible wall, and Lena took it.

"Thanks for letting me stay in touch with Marianne," he said.

"Of course."

He couldn't handle the idea of watching Lena walk away,

so he turned around first and made his way back to his cabin.

Lena was probably watching him go, so he kept his steps upbeat, lying through body language. Only when he was safe in the trees did he allow his shoulders to fall and his steps to slow.

3

J essica leaned up against her bed with her notebook, while Blythe sat at Jessica's desk with a notebook of her own. While Jessica had no interest in becoming an author, she found she didn't mind working away on a scene if she had company. Blythe's dedication was inspiring...plus, Blythe wasn't interested in talking right now, anyway. Jessica had no choice but to work.

Staring at her scribbled-on notebook page, Jessica added a few words to the bottom.

Charlize realized, in that moment, that she was absolutely head over heels in love with Leonardo. It didn't matter that he was a vampire. All that mattered was that they were together.

It was a bit over-the-top, but at least she was on a roll. She was really thinking about love, something she hadn't allowed herself to consider since her freshman year of college. She also knew she had a habit of naming characters after famous movie stars, but she could change the names later if she needed to.

The pull she felt to Leonardo was all-encompassing and over-powering. It was as if a rope had wrapped itself firmly around her heart and tied itself to his heart. And with every breath she took, the rope shortened, the knots growing tighter and tighter.

Scribbling out the part about the rope, she changed it to, *It was as if she was a redwood tree, and he was the sun, and her entire body yearned to stretch up and up so she could bathe in his light.*

Jessica rather liked that. Anything to do with plants, that was her jam.

She had to be with him. There was no other option.

The cabin door burst open, and Jessica squeaked in surprise.

Silhouetted by the late afternoon sunlight was none other than Professor Chaole.

Now *there* was a good villain for Jessica's story.

With her pin-thin eyebrows angling downward, Chaole surveyed the room, her blond bun shaking with her movements. Jessica surveyed the room, too, seeing it with new eyes. Jessica's clothes were strewn everywhere, along with six coffee mugs she'd taken from the kitchen and not yet returned. Three notebooks lay on the floor, one of them open to an ink caricature of Chaole that Jessica had sketched during yesterday's workshop session. Jessica was no artist, but the giant bun and teensy eyebrows were a dead giveaway.

And Blythe sat camped out at Jessica's desk, the bottle of tequila next to her with a shot glass.

Jessica's mouth fell open in horror and she met Blythe's gaze.

They were in deep, deep shit.

"It's not what it looks like—" Jessica began.

"Blythe," Chaole said, her voice a hiss, "pack your things. You'll leave tomorrow morning. Your scholarship is hereby revoked."

No, that wasn't fair at all. Blythe hadn't done anything wrong. At least, no more than Jessica had.

"Please, Professor," Blythe said. "I know I've made a mistake, but we're actually working right now—"

"The rules are clear. We work alone other than during workshop sessions. We do *not* drink. I should have guessed a woman with your background would sneak alcohol into the program."

"Okay, hold on a minute," Jessica said, standing up. "I don't know what the hell that's supposed to mean about her background, but you can't talk to people like this."

Chaole's eyes flashed. "I suggest you stay out of this, Ms. Valdez."

Jessica had spent her teenage and college years following directions, doing as she was told, and staying out of things that weren't her business. And she'd had about enough of that.

"If you make Blythe leave," Jessica said, "I'm going with her."

"Don't be ridiculous." Chaole marched over to the desk and picked up the tequila. She looked down her nose at Blythe.

Blythe lowered her eyes and closed her notebook, her hands shaking.

This was outrageously unfair. They were grown-ass adults. Jessica was tired of being treated like a child. She'd come here to convince her parents to stop hounding her about being an author, but she didn't even owe them that much, honestly.

Chaole continued to glare at Blythe. "Blythe Reimberg, your scholarship is revoked and you will be leaving in the morning. Jessica Valdez, you are free to do whatever you want, but I would recommend against associating with the wrong people."

"The wrong people?" Jessica said, incredulous. "This isn't just about us working in the same room or having alcohol on the premises, is it? It's about Blythe and whatever judgments you're making about her background."

Chaole didn't respond, but Jessica could read the truth in Chaole's mean little eyes.

"*Your* behavior is despicable, not ours. I'll pack my things." Jessica walked up to Chaole and took the tequila from her hand. "And I'm taking my liquor with me."

She didn't wait to see what Chaole did; she simply began gathering her clothes and notebooks.

After several long moments of tense quiet broken only by Chaole's heavy breathing, Chaole turned around and stormed from the room.

Blythe stood frozen next to Jessica's desk, her posture defeated.

Jessica put down her backpack and immediately went to Blythe. "You okay?"

Blythe shook her head. "You don't really have to leave, you know."

"Yes, I really do," Jessica said. "I refuse to be a part of a program that hires an elitist asshole like Chaole. Fuck this place. Go get your things and meet me back here. We'll hike out now and I'll call for a ride as soon as we get cell reception, okay?"

Jessica might be disappointing her parents by not becoming a bestselling author like they wanted her to be, but she knew they'd be proud of her for at least being a decent human being.

∾

THE TRAIL HAD long since disappeared, so Jessica climbed up on a big rock to try for a better view of their surroundings.

"It's going to be dark soon," Blythe pointed out.

"Yeah. Ugh, I'm sorry for dragging you out here. We should've waited for Chaole to call for our transportation." Jessica could hear her mother's admonition. *You need to think before acting. Have a plan, work the plan.* "This is my fault."

"No, I was more than ready to be out of that place," Blythe said. "I would've left tonight, on my own. At least now we have each other."

Jessica pointed to the west, where sunlight reflected off of water. "I see Cougar Lake over there. If we follow along the shore, I bet we pick up a hiking trail that'll take us to a trailhead. And cars. And cell reception."

"Okay," Blythe said. "To the lake."

It didn't take long to reach it, and Blythe gave Jessica a high-five.

"So we'll just circle until we find a trail, sound good?" Jessica asked her.

"Yeah. Let's do this."

By the time they reached the shore, it was dusk, and Jessica was beginning to think this had been a terrible idea. "We're not going to find a trail in the dark like this."

"There's this gravel line," Blythe said, stepping over it.

"True," Jessica said, following her footsteps. "Looks like our best bet, but it would be easy to lose in the dark."

"Yeah." Blythe sighed and sat down on a long flat rock. "I say we try to get comfortable for the night and then find our way in the morning."

It was the best option, so Jessica took a pair of pants from her pack and laid them on the ground. Blythe did the same. Thank goodness it was summer. They might not have the most comfortable night, but at least they wouldn't freeze.

Jessica sat on her makeshift bed and looked out at the lake. "So, here we are. Free."

Blythe snorted. "Yep."

"And...now what?"

"Now, I tell you that you're a fantastic human being." Blythe tapped her chin. "And you break out the tequila."

"Ooh." Jessica found the bottle in her pack. "I mean, it makes sense. To keep warm, right?"

Blythe laughed. "Something like that."

They took turns sipping the tequila and talked long past darkness had completely fallen. Jessica's sides hurt from laughing so hard.

"Nobody's ever given a shit about me, really," Blythe said, "so I meant it when I said you're a fantastic human being."

"Being decent doesn't make me fantastic." Jessica bumped her shoulder into Blythe's.

Blythe bumped her shoulder back. "Well, anyway. Thanks."

"You're welcome."

"And on that note," Blythe said, "I have to pee. Be right back."

"Don't go far," Jessica said.

"I won't."

Jessica listened to her retreating footsteps and the noise of brush as Blythe pushed through it. She hoped the elevation was too high for poison oak, because that was the last thing either of them needed when they got back to civilization. She swore she could get a poison oak rash just from looking at the plant from far away.

A drop landed on her forehead. She looked up, and

several more drops fell on her face. The gentle sound of rain falling on the lake reached her ears, too. Dammit. Rain, really?

And Blythe seemed to be taking a long time for a pee break.

"Blythe?"

She waited, listening. Blythe wasn't the type who would jump out and scare her. It wouldn't be funny at all right now when they were out here on their own.

"Blythe? Please just say something so I know you're okay."

She wasn't sure what possessed her to put on her hiking pack, but she loaded it onto her shoulders. It made her feel bigger, which was nice right now when she was feeling so small.

"Seriously, let me know you're okay," she said again.

The only response was the raindrops hitting the trees and lake. Jessica put her shoulders back. She wasn't going to let a single crappy night get her down.

But what if Blythe had tripped in the darkness and hit her head? She'd need help sooner rather than later.

No more waiting. Jessica had to find her. She tucked her tequila into her pack. Should she bring Jessica's pack, too? It would weigh her down too much, she decided. They could come back for it later. And hopefully all that had happened was Blythe got a little turned around in the dark.

Tightening her pack straps, Jessica strode into the trees in the direction she'd heard Blythe go.

The good thing was that the trees helped shelter her from the rain. The bad thing was that it was darker underneath them.

"Blythe?" Jessica called. "Are you back here?"

No response.

And then she heard the low growl coming from behind her.

She had to have imagined the sound. Because being lost and alone in the woods while it was raining was already bad enough. Adding aggressive wild animals to the mix was too much. The universe wouldn't give her that, too.

Would it?

It would not, she decided as she moved farther into the trees. Yet as her boots sank into the soft earth with every step, she couldn't help but feel as if something was watching her.

She picked up her pace. "It's just my imagination," she muttered. "I'm imagining creepy things because I'm stuck in the creepy woods." Louder, she said, "Blythe! Where are you?"

The growl returned.

She hadn't imagined it.

Something was here with her. Something that wasn't just growling, but giving big, huffing breaths.

Turning, Jessica saw dark eyes and sharp teeth, bared and waiting to strike.

Not knowing what else to do, she ran.

4

Marcus cleaned his fish, unbothered by the darkness or the rain. He'd caught a couple of good ones just before the sun went down, and he was looking forward to a feast.

He'd mostly been able to put the weird interaction with the Junkyard groupie out of his mind, but a part of him couldn't help but wonder how the hell anyone would manage to really keep the groupies out. Would the alphas and witches who'd constructed this place do something about the risk to other shifters—shifters who might try to get into the Junkyard on purpose because they didn't know just how dangerous this place was?

Running footsteps reached his ears, muffled by the rainfall. Probably Jase or Ronan getting their nightly exercise.

Marcus set down the fish he was working on to take a sip from his flask. The flask used to be Carter's, but Marcus had essentially taken over everything that Carter had left behind, including the cabin Carter had built smack in the middle of the Junkyard.

The moonshine in the flask was getting a little low. He'd

soon have to visit Ephraimson, who made it in the back of an old truck. Maybe he could pay Ephraimson in fresh fish.

Along with the footsteps came breathy gasps. That didn't sound like Jase or Ronan. He put down the flask and stood up straight. What was going on?

"Jase?" he said.

The trees were thick to the south side of the lake, so Marcus couldn't see. He walked over, senses on alert. Once in the darkness of the trees, his eyes adjusted and he peered between trunks.

There. Someone running near the outside of the boundary.

A *woman*.

Shit, if this was one of those crazy Junkyard groupies, he had about five seconds to catch her before she stepped over the gravel line and into the Junkyard.

"Hey, cut it out!" he called.

The figure stopped, stumbled. The hiking pack strapped to her shoulders probably upset her balance, and she fell. Picking herself up again, she looked over her shoulder. Her long, dark hair whipped around as she tried to figure out which way to go.

Away, Marcus thought, running forward. *Go away*.

And then he realized—she was already on his side of the gravel line. She'd fallen because she'd rammed right into the invisible wall.

And there was an enraged black bear—not a shifter, but a regular bear—standing a few yards away from her.

Fuck. Fuck. *Fuck*.

"Hold on," Marcus said. "Wait right there, okay? I'm coming to you."

She gasped and started running—right toward Marcus.

He reached out and caught her with his left hand, then

wrapped his right arm around her so she didn't fall again. Her clothes were soaked through, just like his own. She pulled in giant, heaving gasps.

"A...an animal," she said. "I think it hurt my friend. Oh no, I can't believe this..."

The bear ambled over. It stared hard at Marcus, who stared back. He didn't want to fight a normal bear. He didn't want to fight anyone, to be honest. Marcus glared harder, and the bear turned away and ambled off, over the boundary line and into the wilderness beyond the Junkyard.

One crisis averted.

He turned his attention back to the woman in his arms. She smelled like alcohol, although Marcus was pretty sure he didn't smell much better after guzzling Ephraimson's moonshine. He looked desperately around. If there was ever a good time for Jase to show up on that run, now would be it. Marcus could pawn this groupie off on Jase and...

He sniffed again.

She wasn't a Junkyard groupie. She was *human*.

Quadruple fuck. He tried to let go of her, but she'd latched onto his arm.

"Look, I can't help you," he said.

"Please—my friend, you don't understand—there was an *animal*."

He understood better than she did. "Let me get you somewhere safe, and then I can look for your friend."

"I should help you, we can look together."

"Um, no. That's not going to work. Do you think you're going to find anything out here in the dark?"

"No." She lifted her gaze to his and looked into his face for the first time. Her chocolate brown eyes nearly took his breath away. "You swear you'll come back out for her?"

"I swear."

He owed this woman nothing, and yet he knew he'd be out here as soon as he got her settled somewhere safe. Not his cabin—it was too much in the middle of things, and someone would eventually notice her scent.

Remembering the old trailer at the north of the Junkyard, he nodded to himself. That was the best place for her. It was out of the way. Marcus, Lena, and Kyle had all stayed there when they first came to the Junkyard, and it would be the perfect spot to hide this woman away. Grant and Caitlyn could help keep an eye on her until they figured out how to get her out of here.

"Come with me," he said. "Do you want me to carry your pack?"

"No, I'm fine." She held fast to his arm, making it harder to walk than it needed to be.

"You're going to have to let me go," Marcus said.

"Can I hold your hand, then?" she asked.

His heart clenched, and suddenly he'd like nothing more than to hold her hand. Weird, because he didn't even know her, yet her fear must have activated his protective instincts or something.

"Sorry," she said after a moment, "I know it sounds so stupid when I say it out loud—"

"You can hold my hand, but not on that side. The hand's gone."

"Oh. Okay."

He guided her to his left side and gripped her hand. "Let's go—there's a trailer where you can stay, and it should be safe enough."

"Where are we?" she asked. "A campground?"

"Something like that."

He'd have to explain it to her, but now wasn't the time. Not when she was at least a little drunk and he was too, and she was worried about her friend. And any moment, another shifter could show up and discover her.

As they walked, fat raindrops dripped on their heads through the pine branches above.

"So where are we?" she asked.

"We need to be quiet," he said. "We don't want to attract the animals."

She gasped and whispered, "Animals? Plural?"

"Yeah."

It took longer than it normally would to reach the trailer. She tripped frequently, although she never fell. The muddy ground wasn't helping. Plus he knew from his half-sister that humans had much worse night vision than shifters did. When Marianne was little, she used to test his abilities, asking him to turn off all the lights when he put her to bed. Then she'd throw random objects through her dark room to see if he could catch them.

Marianne had grown up thinking that having Marcus for a brother was the same as having a big fluffy dog.

It was his life's mission to make sure she never saw him as the monster he truly was.

"What's your name?" the woman holding his hand asked. "I should tell you...I don't go home with men I don't know."

"You're not going home with me," Marcus said. "This place will be yours. But my name's Marcus."

"Jessica," she said.

"It's nice to meet you." But it would've been a fuck-ton nicer under different circumstances.

They reached the trailer and Marcus steered her around to the front, which faced not the Junkyard, but the boundary line. Rain pattered loudly against the trailer's metal roof.

"I love the sound of rain," Jessica mumbled.

He opened the door for her and peeked inside to make sure all was as he'd left it when he moved out. A strong whiff of Lena's and Kyle's scents filled his nose, and he grieved all over again for Kyle's death and Lena leaving the Junkyard.

"There are blankets in there," he said to Jessica, "so you can get tucked in. Do not come out, okay? It's dangerous out here for you. So just wait until I come back."

"You're really going to find my friend?" she asked, hesitating in the doorway.

"I'm going to try. What's her name?"

"Blythe."

"Okay," he said. "I'll be back soon."

"Thanks."

She went inside and he shut the door behind her. If he could bar the door, even better. He didn't know why, but he was personally invested in keeping her safe.

He also wanted to talk to her, learn more about her life. But there was no time. He turned around and ran back to the place where he'd found her. If Blythe was nearby, he needed to get to her as quickly as possible. Better Marcus finding them both than the other shifters. Not everyone in the Junkyard was a total asshole, but he'd heard stories about some of those other guys, and he'd seen what some of them were capable of.

When he reached the lake, he kept going past the fish he'd abandoned and toward the boundary line that curved against the shore. The boundary extended out into the water. Marcus knew he wasn't the only miserable sonuvabitch who'd tried swimming out there and getting past the boundary. But even in the water, the invisible wall remained.

Fucking witches, they thought of everything.

At least the territory had water, he supposed, and sometimes decent fishing.

The rain had washed away most of the scents of Jessica and anyone else who might've come into the territory with her. He went all the way to the gravel line and sniffed carefully, even getting on his hand and knees. Irritated when he couldn't smell anything, he took off his clothes and shifted into his wolf. His gait was different, now that he had lost his right forepaw, but he got along well enough.

Jessica's scent was flowery and sweet like freesia. He picked it up, faint over the gravel and the ground nearby. A second, even fainter scent, touched his nose. Also sweet, but fruity instead of flowery.

He followed the second scent for a few yards, until he realized where it was headed. It was going straight into the dump—the part of the Junkyard where assholes like Barnum and Alleman lived.

And her scent was mixed with a shifter's. Alleman's, if he wasn't mistaken.

Fuck. He needed to get back to Jessica. But he couldn't leave this other woman behind, especially not if Alleman had her. Following the fruity scent, he made his way toward the dump.

He kept his head low to the ground, his paws soft against the rain-soaked earth. He hadn't gone far before he saw the very thing he'd feared—Alleman holding a struggling form, his hand pressed over her mouth to keep her quiet.

Marcus held in the growl of outrage building in his chest. He launched himself forward, intent on Alleman's legs. If Marcus knocked Alleman over, he could hold him by the throat and give Blythe a chance to run...but run where? He'd worry about that later, once she was free.

Now he was three yards away from Alleman, who still hadn't noticed him approaching. Two yards away. One.

Bam. Something slammed into Marcus's side. He hadn't smelled the leopard shifter in the rain, but Barnum, in his cat form, had already wrapped his sinewy body around Marcus and was kicking hard, raking Marcus's side with his powerful hind legs.

Blindly, Marcus bit down on the closest thing he could reach, which turned out to be Barnum's foreleg. Barnum snarled and hissed, then pulled back.

Before Marcus could recover, Barnum swatted his face with a giant paw, claws running over his skin. Marcus felt his eye immediately swell closed.

Shit, this was going downhill fast. He scrambled back to assess the situation and figure out where Alleman was taking Blythe. Barnum gave him no view, immediately jumping at him again.

Marcus's side ached, his face ached, and he could only see out of one eye. Still, he dodged Barnum's attack.

Barnum attacked again, this time from Marcus's left, where he had limited visibility. Marcus jerked away.

He wasn't fast enough—Barnum got him by the throat.

Resisting at this point was futile, unless Marcus wanted his throat ripped out. Barnum's dominance was established. Fuck. When Marcus didn't immediately signify yielding by relaxing his muscles, Barnum growled.

Letting loose a growl of his own, Marcus relaxed.

Barnum let go of his neck.

Alleman still held the struggling woman. He looked bored. "Better luck next time, One-hand."

Several more guys came out of the shadows. Marcus shifted back to human, wincing at the pain radiating through his face.

"Fuck, now everyone saw her," Alleman said.

"What's with the chick?" someone asked.

The woman in question had red hair made darker by the rain. Her eyes blazed not with fear, but with fury. It was a good thing Alleman had such a good grip on her, because in a fight between the two of them, Marcus wasn't sure Alleman would come out standing. Blythe looked pissed enough to best him if only she could get free.

Alleman seemed to be thinking. "I haven't decided what to do with her yet. I don't want to be out in this fuckin' rain anymore."

"And meanwhile, who gets her?" the guy asked.

"Finders keepers?" Alleman suggested.

"No one gets her." It was Jase who spoke up as he leaned against an old upright piano. "Only seems fair, right? Until we can decide what to do with her?"

There were enough murmurs of support that Alleman's shoulders fell in defeat.

"I'll put her somewhere safe," Alleman grumbled.

At least Alleman and Barnum wouldn't be able to hurt her now. If nothing else, Marcus's interference meant that every shifter in the Junkyard now knew about Blythe's presence.

The other shifters followed Alleman as he carried Blythe farther into the dump.

Jase came over to Marcus and held out a hand to help him up.

Marcus took it and muttered, "Thanks."

"No problem."

When Jase just stood there facing him, Marcus said, "Watch out for her. Make sure they put her somewhere safe."

"Good call."

His face hurt like hell. His ribs, too; Barnum had cracked one.

He limped back the way he'd come until he reached his clothes. They were soaked through, so he picked them up and went back to his cabin. There, he pulled on a clean pair of jeans and a dry thermal. The rain had slowed, but hadn't stopped all the way. The dry interior of his cabin was tempting.

But he pushed his way outside, leaving the comfort of his cabin behind. He had to get back to Jessica, make sure she was safe and not wandering around on this cold, drizzly night.

5

Jessica woke up warm and dry, grateful that last night's misadventure had been a dream and she was safe in her writing cabin.

Any minute, the camp's bells would start chiming to rouse everyone for breakfast.

She waited, keeping her eyes closed for a few more blissful moments before she'd have to see Chaole. She stretched and turned over...and knocked into someone else.

Her eyes snapped open. A broad back faced her, a faded gray long-sleeved thermal shirt stretched across it. The neck attached to the back led up to a head of shaggy brown hair.

This wasn't anyone from her writing intensive.

And this wasn't her cabin.

Scrambling away from the stranger in this strange bed, she tried to take the blanket with her. Unfortunately, the guy was sleeping on top of the blanket. The fabric wouldn't move. She draped it over her lap as she took stock of her body. Clothes were on, everything except for her shoes. She sat up on her knees to peer over the giant blocking her from the rest of this...trailer.

That's right. She was in a camp trailer. She remembered, now. A man had helped her—this man. He'd made her feel safe and he'd promised to find Blythe.

But there was no Blythe in sight.

"Hey," she said, shoving her palm against his back.

He rumbled something in that deep, gruff voice he had, a voice that was almost a growl. Despite the circumstances, she found herself really liking his voice. It made her want to pay attention to every word he said.

"Hey, wake up." She shoved him again. "Where's Blythe?"

He turned around to face her and she gasped. One entire side of his face was bruised and covered in healing cuts. More bruises surrounded one of his eyes, which was swollen. Had his face been like this last night? She couldn't remember. It had been difficult to see in the dark, anyway.

"What happened to your face?" she asked.

He sat up. "Nothing."

"It's *something*, obviously," she said, coming around to his side to get a better view.

He turned his face away again.

"Dammit, Mike," she said.

"I'm not Mike."

"Your name starts with an M, I can remember that much, Melvin."

He shook his head.

"Malik. Matthew. Mason. Whatever. *Where is my friend*?"

"She's alive," he said finally, staring at the opposite side of the trailer. "I couldn't get to her, though."

"Do we need to call Search and Rescue? Why have we not already done this? Why didn't you wake me up when you got back?"

He laughed.

"Okay, asshole," she said, pushing on his shoulder and trying to climb off the weird trailer bed. She'd take care of things herself. She just hoped Blythe was okay.

He took up the entire area where she should be able to get out of bed, and he wasn't budging.

"Move it," she said.

"We need to talk."

"Sure, Mateo. Let me out of here and we can talk while we call emergency services and help Blythe."

She tried to scramble around his torso, but he held up his arm and blocked her. His arm was strong and muscled, but his hand was gone. She remembered him mentioning that last night.

Growling in irritation, she said, "Why the hell won't you let me out of here?"

"Because you can't get out," he said simply. "No one can."

She shook her head. "That makes absolutely no sense."

"Look," he said, twisting sideways to face her once more, "it's complicated. Do you believe in magic?"

Folding her arms across her chest, she glared at him. "You've got to be fucking kidding me."

"Fuck." He looked to the ceiling, as if searching for patience. She hoped he found extra, because she could use some, too. "Okay, here's the thing. There's a boundary that we can't get over. It's like an invisible wall. It keeps people in this area."

"Riiiiight," she said slowly. "Okay, well, my dad always tells me that obstacles are ninety percent mental, so while you believe you're trapped in this trailer, I know for a fact I can walk out of here as soon as I—climb—around—you—mountain-muscle-man."

Every time she tried to squeeze past him, he blocked her. What a super jerk. She should have been frightened, but he didn't make her feel afraid. She felt safe. Just confused and annoyed. She needed to find Blythe. Why wasn't he letting her?

"I have to get my friend," she said. "Let me out of here."

His voice was calm, despite her growing impatience. "I'll let you out in just a second. First you need to understand what's going on here. And I will personally help you get your friend, but no rescue operation is going to do any good because of the underlying problem of this territory."

She sat back on her feet and stared at him. His bruises seemed to be fading, a trick of the morning light. The scruff on his jaw looked scratchy and tempting, so different from what she was used to seeing on the guys she spent time with. She'd always dated clean-cut boys. Boys her parents would approve of. Boys who could wear a tux and unironically order a martini shaken, not stirred.

There was no moving him, so she'd cooperate with his crazy talk until it was possible to sneak past. "Fine. Tell me about this quote-unquote underlying problem."

"You don't believe me, so I'm going to show you. Can you please trust me for five minutes and...and try not to freak out?"

"Fine."

"Good." He got up.

Not waiting for a second, she scrambled off of the bed, pushed him behind her, and took five running steps to the door of the camp trailer.

He was immediately next to her; she hadn't even seen him move. But he didn't touch her, didn't try to restrain her. He simply reached around her waist to unlatch the door.

Before she could bolt outside, though, he said, "Please don't run. There are some bad guys in these woods. If you run, it'll make it hard for me to protect you."

He sounded genuinely worried. It made her stop and think. His face was all bashed up after he'd gone out to find Blythe last night.

"Okay," she said. "I'll stand right here."

He sniffed the air, which was weird, then said, "Good."

She stepped out of the trailer and he followed her.

Taking her hand, he led her toward a line of gravel. She focused on the tiny plants poking through the carpet of pine needles and along the edge of the gravel, trying not to think about how good it felt to have his fingers intertwined with hers. What was wrong with her? She'd just met this man and he was nothing like the guys she usually dated.

Then again, every other guy she'd dated had just about bored her to tears. Or they'd been dating her because of her parents. Maybe, after she got out of this place, it would be time to date someone a little different.

The pine needles were still wet from last night's rain, so she had to concentrate on not slipping.

"Stop here," he said. "See this line?"

She followed the line with her eyes. "I see it, yep."

"It's the barrier. We can't leave."

She couldn't hold in her laugh. "Look, Miguel, I don't know why you think that, but here—"

She put out a hand to show him there was no barrier.

Her hand met something solid.

"What the heck?" she muttered, trying again. And again her palm stopped against an invisible wall. It was cool to the touch, and smooth. She let go of the guy's hand that held her right one and used both of her hands to touch the barrier.

"So," he said, "magic is real. Like I told you. And we should go get your friend, but we don't have a way for the two of you to get out of here."

"It's like this all over?" she asked, following the gravel line, her hand out to run against the invisible barrier as she walked.

"Yes. Most of us in here have walked the boundary more than once, just like you're doing."

"Give me a boost," she said.

He sighed. "We can't get over it, either."

"Give me a boost, Mitch."

Bending down, he grabbed her around the legs and lifted her up so she sat on his shoulder. He steadied her when she wobbled, his right arm against her thigh. Scars covered the part of his arm where his wrist should've started. How long ago had he lost his hand?

None of her business, she reminded herself. Planting one of her hands on top of his head for extra balance, she reached out with her other. The wall extended high, past her reach, and it felt like it started to curve inward, as well.

"We're in a freaking *dome*?" she asked.

"That's what we think."

"Why? Why is this here?"

He didn't respond right away.

"You can let me down," Jessica said.

"Right."

She held onto his shoulders as he bent, then twisted around as he lowered her. When she reached the ground, her front was pressing against his. Heat flared throughout her body. Wow, this dude ran warm.

Stepping back quickly, she asked again, "So, why is this invisible wall here?"

"We call this place the Junkyard, and it's for certain kinds of people who can't get along with their groups."

She frowned. Certain kinds of people. Groups. He was being purposefully vague. "Mikhail, if you don't tell me what the hell is going on in three seconds, I'm going to lose my shit."

"This place is like a prison for shapeshifters," he said. "And my name is not Mikhail."

"Shapeshifters," she said, folding her arms across her chest. This was unbelievable. But so was an invisible wall. Maybe she'd imagined that. She backed up a little bit until her ass couldn't go any farther. Turning around, she saw nothing behind her.

Nope, hadn't imagined it. There was a wall, and it was invisible.

"Yeah," he said. "Like werewolves."

"Are you going to prove shapeshifters to me now, too?" she asked, taking an exaggerated look at the woods surrounding them. "Do you have one hidden around somewhere, maybe under the bed in the trailer?"

He pointed to his chest. "I have one in here."

Jessica struggled not to laugh.

"You don't have to believe me," he said. "It would be better in some ways if you didn't. But the fact remains, there are some bad guys trapped in here with us. They aren't all bad, but enough of them are that you should stay put."

"And Blythe is out there with the bad guys? I don't know what kind of friend you are, but I'm a better friend than that."

"No." He huffed in impatience. "I'll go get her."

"Like you tried to get her last night."

His dark gray eyes filled with pain, and she immediately felt bad.

"I tried, yeah," he said.

"I'm sorry. Thank you for trying." She met his eyes while she said it, so he could see her sincerity. The swelling around his eye was going down, and the bruising over his cheek was fading—in fact, it was nearly entirely gone. "What happened to your black eye, though? It's like it never happened."

He shrugged. "I heal fast."

"Nobody heals that fast."

"Shifters do."

In the years of trying to sort real friends from the fake ones who just wanted to get closer to her parents, Jessica had honed some ability to figure out when people weren't being genuine. And nothing about this guy was setting off her alarm bells. Yet the things he said were *impossible*.

She had to let it go. She'd already wasted enough time with words.

"Will you try to get her again?" she asked him.

"I will. But you have to stay here."

She opened her mouth to argue, but he held up his hand. "If you believe nothing else that I've told you just now, believe this. A woman in this territory of what is essentially a big pack of prisoners is a terrible idea. We can't let them know you're here."

His words were chilling. Jessica had never tried to be courageous in her life. There had never been any need. Yet she hated herself more than a little when she nodded at the guy and said, "Fine, Mack. You can go on your own."

"Thanks, James," he said. "It means a lot that you can trust me."

As he walked away, she mouthed the name *James* at his back. Had the gruff mountain of a man made a joke?

6

W hen Marcus was far enough away from the trailer, he exhaled. Deeply. Being around that woman made him tense. Not in a bad way. More in a throat-choked-up, she-deserves-better kind of way.

She was a human woman, stuck in the Junkyard.

And her friend was in here, too.

He wanted to help them both, but his protective wolf tendencies were going into overdrive just from being around Jessica. Even now, his inner wolf was going crazy because he was walking away from her.

She *wanted* him to go, though. She was sending him on a mission.

The wolf didn't care. The wolf wanted to be close to her, protect her, provide for her.

It hadn't been an accident that Marcus had held Jessica's hand when she tried pushing her hand against the boundary. Given the strong vibes his wolf was giving off, he'd thought maybe—just maybe—she could be his mate.

Maybe the wall would let her out of the Junkyard, and possibly him as well.

Maybe he could see his sister again.

But of course it hadn't worked. Marcus couldn't have a mate. He was broken on the inside—the last year had seen to that. If he'd been whole, he would've seen Vince's pursuit of his sister much earlier, and seen it for the twisted abuse it was. He'd have intervened before it got so bad, and he would've planned ahead, taken care of it in a way that didn't hurt his pack. If he'd done it right, Vince would be the one in the Junkyard, alive and breathing. If he'd done it right, Marcus would be free.

Now he could never go back to his pack.

But Jessica wasn't here for him, anyway. She and her friend hadn't come into the Junkyard to hook up with bad guys. And every man in here was here for a reason.

He skirted around the edge of the pond. Past that, he came to a rocky area that looked like it had served as a quarry way back in the day. Now he was approaching the dump, where most of the Junkyard shifters had their dens.

He tallied the guys he was most worried about. Barnum and Alleman after last night, for sure. Buenevista and Mollin were both assholes, but they hadn't been around much lately.

Mathers was dead, thank fuck, but Barnum had been formed from the same mold.

Past the quarry, he breathed a little easier, because he was past Alleman's den. Old vehicles sat scattered in clumps like a giant had thrown them in a game of dice. A few grasses and trees rose up, fighting to make life amidst the scraps of industrial machinery.

He tried to pick up the scent of Jessica's friend, but couldn't. Where had they taken her last night? Next he tried scenting Barnum, who smelled like wet earth, but Barnum's scent was mixed in with everyone else's. Without any scents to go by, Marcus would be searching the old-fashioned way, with his eyes.

He stopped short when he came around the skeleton of a giant tractor and saw an old RV squished up close to the tractor's opposite wheel well. The RV hadn't been here before, and tracks in the mud showed someone had dragged it over. It had a broken window on the passenger side—too small for anyone to get in or out.

While he stood there, something moved inside the RV. Then it went still again. He looked around, sniffed the air, couldn't smell much. Slowly, carefully, he approached the RV.

A pile of concrete blocks blocked the driver's door. He walked around to the front of the RV, and the window up there was covered in a giant piece of sheet metal.

They'd made a cage for her? That was his only guess—that Blythe was inside the RV.

He had to get closer if he was going to talk to her. Going back around to the passenger side of the RV, he clambered over the old tractor.

"Blythe?" he whispered.

In response, a metal pipe appeared out of the window and clocked him in the forehead.

"Ow, fuck," he said, falling on his ass into the tractor seat.

"Back the fuck up," a feminine voice said, "or I'll whack you again."

He stared at the window but could only see shadows.

A few yards away, someone chuckled. Marcus turned to look, rubbing his head. He saw a head of dark hair, a wide smile, and tanned skin. Jase, a mountain lion shifter, was laughing at Marcus. Figured. The asshole found everything funny.

Marcus flipped him off and turned back to the RV. Quietly, so Jase couldn't hear him, he said, "I'm here because of Jessica. She wants me to make sure you're okay."

Silence from the RV. Then the woman said, "Other than a bunch of stinky creepers talking about who gets to be my *mate*, I'm fine and dandy, thanks. Always wanted to live in an RV and play whack-a-mole with guys' heads."

He took a step toward the van, but the metal pipe appeared in the window again.

"Don't even think about it, douche-wad. You could be lying about Jessica."

"True," he said. "But I'm not here to hurt you."

"Refreshing," she said in a wry voice.

"Do you want out of there?" he asked.

"Like it would do any good," she said. "I spent half the night banging into an invisible brick wall. So if you have a way through that, come back and let me know."

So she already knew about the magic to some extent. Good. "Yeah, I'm working on that," he said. "I'll let you know. I'll come back later with food."

"No need. Some other douche-wad is already taking care of it. I hate you all, you know."

He could hear the truth in her words, and it seemed fair enough. "All right. I'll see you later, then."

She didn't respond, but he caught a flash of orange-red hair before she returned to the shadows.

Jase's laughter caught his attention again, so Marcus went around the RV to see him.

"She's a piece of work," Jase said, jerking his chin toward the RV. His gold and green eyes were shining with humor.

Marcus rubbed his forehead. "Ya think? How'd she get herself barricaded in there?"

"Alleman was using it as a little cage for her. That backfired when she grabbed the pipe and started hitting him."

"Nice," Marcus said.

"Barnum and Alleman are organizing a big battle to 'win' her."

"When?"

Jase clenched his jaw. "Two weeks."

"That's a long time."

"They're trying to make it into a big thing," Jase said. "Build up suspense and let people train up for it. But I'm not going to let it happen."

"There's only one of you," Marcus said.

"I'm not the only decent bastard in this Junkyard."

Marcus scoffed. "So, what, you're going to form an alliance? The Junkyard Shifters United?"

"I'll start a pride if I have to."

Well, good luck to him, trying to get this crew of misfits into something resembling a shifter group. Marcus would believe it when he saw it.

Two weeks until the fight, though. Well, it would allow him time to figure out how to get Jessica and her friend out of the Junkyard.

"You're bringing her food?" he said to Jase.

"Yeah. I have to dodge that pipe of hers every time. She's strong."

"Good luck." Marcus walked away, rubbing his head. He wasn't sure how Jessica was going to feel about any of this, but it seemed to him that Blythe was safe enough for now.

Actually, he could guess how Jessica would feel—she'd be pissed that he wasn't coming back with Blythe. And rightly so. Trying to explain the Junkyard and its rules and dangers to a human who hadn't even believed in magic until this morning was impossible.

At least Jase was feeding Blythe. Which reminded Marcus that he should bring some food to Jessica. She had to be hungry—Marcus was, too.

He stopped at his cabin and opened up the ice chest that had been delivered a few days ago. After putting several things into a sack, he left again.

He came back to the trailer, but instead of going inside to see Jessica like his wolf wanted him to do, he walked the few extra yards to the barrier and looked toward the cabin outside. He didn't see Grant or Caitlyn, but both of their cars were in the drive.

Picking up a small rock, he hoisted it to throw at the side of the cabin. Just before he tossed it, though, Grant came out of the garage. His light brown hair was neatly trimmed, unlike Marcus's darker hair, which was starting to fall into his eyes. The mountain lion shifter was messy in other ways, though; he was a painter and streaks and splotches of different colors stained his hands, arms, and clothes.

"Grant," Marcus called.

Grant turned immediately, changing his trajectory from his cabin door and over to Marcus at the barrier. He nodded at Marcus. "How's it going?"

"I need a witch."

Frowning, Grant said, "The only reason someone in the Junkyard wants a witch is to get past that wall."

"It's not for me," Marcus said. "Two humans got through last night. We need to get them out before the others harm them."

Grant rubbed the back of his neck and shook his head. "Damn. I'll do what I can, of course, but the witch, Maddie, didn't seem all that concerned with Caitlyn's plight when

Caitlyn got stuck in there. She only agreed to help us if we could get a white crystal from the quarry for her."

"I can get a white crystal," Marcus said.

Grant shrugged. "You can try. I don't know that it'll work, necessarily."

That didn't sound reassuring at all. "But the witch helped you two get out," Marcus said.

"Not exactly," Grant said.

Marcus remembered how Lena and Carter had simply walked over the gravel line, as if nothing had been keeping them inside at all.

"Mates," Marcus said.

Grant nodded.

Of course. It always came down to that. Which wasn't helpful. Marcus had already tried that. Besides, even if for some crazy reason the fates decided that Marcus was able to have a mate, and that mate was Jessica...what about Blythe?

"But you'll get in touch with the witch for me?" Marcus asked.

"I'll definitely try. Is there anything else you need over there?"

He'd need about ten tons of patience if he was heading into the trailer to talk to Jessica, but he doubted Grant had spare patience lying around. "Nah, I'm good."

"The humans," Grant said. "Are they women?"

Marcus nodded.

"Caitlyn got some condoms for Carter," Grant said.

"Yeah." Marcus had found them in the cabin. "What does that have to do with anything?"

"Well, Marcus, when two people like each other very much and want to bang it out—"

"Okay, I got it," Marcus said, realizing what Grant was talking about. "Neither of these women is here for that."

"If it turns out they are," Grant said, "make sure they're as safe as possible. Remember the condoms."

"Sure, okay, Dad."

Grant laughed and walked away. Marcus was left alone. Jessica was in the trailer behind him; he could hear her puttering around in there, her footsteps projecting anxiety. He should go in, reassure her that Blythe was okay.

Problem was, nobody was okay. This was so messed up. These Sierra mountains were the prettiest place on earth, with their towering evergreens and the wildflowers blooming in the sun-saturated clearings. A goshawk flew overhead, screaming *ki-ki-ki-ki* as it swooped in pursuit of prey.

Marcus deserved to be here, and he could appreciate the beauty in his surroundings along with the sharp pang of knowing he could never leave. But Jessica and Blythe deserved freedom.

Sighing, he spun around and marched up to the camp trailer.

"Hey, Micah," Jessica said when he walked in.

He tried not to smile—her constant guesses at his name were endearing. "Hey, Janice."

She went on without missing a beat, "Did you talk to Blythe?"

"Yep. She's safe."

"Good. Did she say anything? Also, I hope you don't mind that I made some instant coffee—"

He stepped the rest of the way into the camp trailer. "Look, here's the thing with Blythe. You're not going to like it."

7

Jessica stared at the guy. Something in his face told her she might want to sit down for this news.

She didn't want bad news. The day had not been great. She'd spent hours feeling bored, and a lot of time in denial. She'd messed with her phone for ages, trying to get a signal of any kind, but without any luck. And then, her phone's battery ran out as a final *fuck you* to Jessica's current predicament.

The one good thing was the trailer. It was tiny and cramped, but cozy. The jalousie windows had thin curtains covering them, and the cushions around the dining table were a cheerful red.

Cozy or not, she didn't want to hear bad news.

"Is this a good news slash bad news thing," she asked, "where there are two sides to it? Because if there's anything good, I want that news first."

"She's safe for the moment," he said.

Jessica leaned heavily against the counter, gripping it in her hands. "Okay, so that is good."

He didn't say anything else, but she could sense his gaze on her face, so she looked up.

His expression was hungry, lustful. But that couldn't be right.

"What is it?" she asked.

He looked away quickly and ran a hand over the scruff on his jaw and chin. "Nothing."

"Then put me out of suspense. What's the bad news?"

"Some of the guys here want to fight for her."

She narrowed her eyes at him. "Fight for her...how? Why?"

"They want to win her. To claim her as their own."

"Whether she wants to be won or not," Jessica guessed.

He nodded.

"That's sick," she said. "Like she's a piece of property. Women are *not* property."

He nodded again.

"I have to go to her." Jessica no longer cared about the cups of instant coffee resting on the tiny counter.

"You can't do that," he said.

"Screw that." She started forward, but he blocked her way. "Why are you being such a bully?"

"It's for your own safety because you keep insisting on doing stupid shit," he growled.

"I'm going to kick you in the nuts if you don't move in five...four...three...two...one."

He didn't move. She wondered if he thought he was fast enough to block her kick, but it didn't really matter, because she wasn't going to kick him, anyway.

"How did you know I wouldn't kick you?" she asked.

"I can sense dishonesty." He shrugged, like that wasn't some huge revelation.

"Well, I can't sense dishonesty," she said, "and I hate all

these half-assed answers. So can you tell me what's going on here? Really?"

"Get your coffee and come outside with me."

"You don't get to order me around." She stuck her tongue out at his back as he left the trailer, but she grabbed not only her mug, but the one she'd poured for him, and she followed him outside.

He faced her, his gray eyes soft and looking surprisingly gentle against the rough whiskers on his face. His bruises were completely gone, except for what looked like a fresh one on his forehead.

"Take your damn coffee," she said. She'd been so proud of getting the burner to work.

He took the mug from her, but he didn't take a sip. Instead he stared directly into her eyes and said, "Everything I told you before is true. Every single thing."

"So you're telling me that marching off to rescue my friend would be the equivalent of the blond teenager running into the haunted house in a horror movie?"

He cocked his head. "Not how I would've worded it, but yeah."

There was no bullshit in what he was saying.

She went on, "But she's safe right now. Blythe, I mean. She's truly okay?"

"Yes." He pointed to the new bruise on his forehead. "She gave me this, in fact. She's pretty well set up to defend herself for the next while, and someone's bringing her food."

Jessica's stomach growled. "Speaking of food, Magnus, do you have any?"

"I do. I brought all this with me." He waved his arm toward a bag on the ground.

She didn't care how shameless it made her look—she set

the cup down immediately and dove for the bag, taking everything out—a loaf of bread, some peanut butter, and a few apples.

Taking an apple in her hand, she bit into it, letting the sweet taste burst over her tongue. "Ohmygosh, I think I love you," she said.

His gray gaze darkened, and she rolled her eyes. If he couldn't handle a little hyperbole, then he wouldn't be able to handle being her friend.

Her friend? She didn't know this guy.

But anyone who'd bring her food when she was starving...well, okay, he was a friend. She was a simple woman with simple needs.

She took a few more bites of the apple, wiping juice from her chin with the back of her wrist. Then she looked up at the guy again.

"Why did we have to come out here for you to tell me all this stuff?" she asked.

He smirked. "You want the truth?"

"Yes?" She said it like a question, because his smirk made her think maybe she didn't want the truth after all.

"Because being in that little trailer with you, and your scent filling my nostrils, is making me think naughty things."

She felt her eyebrows move up toward her hairline. "What?"

He shrugged. "It's the truth."

Of all the frickin' nerve. She couldn't help but like what he'd said, but she didn't want him to know that. "Do you want to be wearing my coffee right now?"

"Seems a shame to waste it," he said.

She went inside the trailer to throw away her apple core. Turning around to go back out, she paused on the threshold to the trailer. The guy was looking at the ground, as if he was ashamed of something.

"Michael?" Jessica said. "You okay?"

"I apologize for being crude," he said.

Well, if that wasn't the most adorable thing.

"I've forgotten how to flirt," he added.

She felt bad for him. If he wanted to flirt with her, she didn't entirely mind. Even while she recognized this was hardly the place to be flirting, well, what the heck else was she going to do while she was stuck?

"It helps when there's alcohol," she said.

Taking a step closer to her, he said, "Are you telling me you want some flirting?"

"Um." She bit her lip. "I'm not saying anything. Except I have some tequila in my backpack."

Going back into the trailer, she found her backpack and pulled the tequila from it. The giant bottle was three quarters full, even after sipping from it yesterday with Blythe.

Just yesterday, she thought. That was when their biggest problem had been an asshole professor and the need to get cell reception to call for a ride into town.

The stark difference between yesterday and today hit her suddenly, and she felt her knees go weak. Her eyes filled with tears. What was she doing, getting tequila when she should be railing against that stupid invisible wall that she'd spent most of her day smacking and kicking? Eventually it had to give, didn't it?

The tequila bottle clunked on the linoleum floor of the trailer and she crouched down next to it, wrapping her arms around her knees. She closed her eyes and wondered if she'd ever get up.

She knew she was being melodramatic, but she couldn't find it in herself to care. This place didn't make any sense.

People didn't get stuck in invisible bubble worlds full of magical creatures.

What was going to happen to her?

"Hey, I got you." Warm arms came around her, along with an earthy, mossy scent.

"I want to go home," she said.

He went still and said, "Jacqueline, remember how I can scent dishonesty?"

"Yeah."

"Well," he said, "what you said isn't true. I don't know why you don't want to go home, but you don't."

"Oh. I guess you're right." She sniffled. Home would suck, too; there, she would be stuck for entirely different reasons. She'd have to explain to her parents why she was out of the writing program. She'd have to convince them not to enroll her in another, despite the fact she was a college graduate with her own interests that didn't revolve around writing fiction. "I don't even know what I want. Except I do know that I don't want to be stuck in this place."

"Yeah, you and me both, Jones."

She couldn't help the little laugh that escaped her. "What's your name, really?"

"Marcus."

"I knew it started with an M," she said with satisfaction. "Do you want to know my name?"

"It's Jessica," he said simply.

She laughed and shook her head. "You mean you knew all along?"

"Yeah, I just thought it was funny to pretend I didn't."

"Jerk."

"Hey, you really didn't know my name, and you just called me whatever." He tightened his arms around her and she let his heat soothe her. She had no idea why this near-stranger's hug was such a comfort, but she'd take advantage of it while it lasted.

"Is there anything I can do to help you right now?" he asked, sitting back.

She frowned, not liking the new distance or the cool air that took his place against her skin.

"Short of taking you to Blythe," he added, "which would be a disaster on so many levels, including the fact she might smack the hell out of you with her metal pipe."

Jessica couldn't help the smile stretching across her face at the thought of Blythe wielding a pipe.

"I guess what I need," she said, "is to know what our plan is. How are we getting through that barrier?"

He reached for the tequila. "May I?"

Jessica nodded. He held the bottle in the crook of his right arm and used his left hand to unscrew the top.

His lips tilted in a smile as he held the bottle up. "Cheers."

After he took a swig, he passed the bottle to Jessica. She took a small sip, then gave it back to Marcus.

"Damn, that shit's good," he said, then took another sip. "Then again, all I've had the past month is Noah Ephraimson's moonshine, so anything else would seem good in comparison."

Jessica took the bottle back and swallowed a bigger gulp.

"So," Marcus said. "Our plan. It isn't a great one, but it's all I've got so far. A witch made this barrier wall, so it stands to reason a witch could help us through it."

"Makes sense," Jessica said. The alcohol was already starting to affect her, probably because all she'd eaten today was that apple. "I should have a sandwich."

"Wait here, I'll bring the stuff in and make you one," he said.

That was oddly sweet. She got up, too, but only to sit at the tiny table at one end of the trailer.

Marcus came back inside, carrying the bag. She watched as he made her sandwich.

"Thanks," she said when he set it in front of her on a plate.

He made one for himself, too, and he slid into the space across from her at the table.

"What happened to your hand?" Jessica blurted, then covered her mouth. "I'm so sorry. It isn't my business. You don't have to answer me."

He picked up his sandwich. "I don't mind. I lost it a couple of months ago. Fight with another shifter."

Jessica blinked. "That recently? It looks all healed up, like it's been years."

"That's part of being a shifter," he said. "Fast healing, remember? We fight so much, we'd probably be extinct if it wasn't for the fast healing."

"Wow." She didn't know what to think about all the shifter talk, but she'd roll with it, for now.

"Anyway, so the witch," Marcus went on. "I have a friend on the outside and he's going to get in touch with her for me. She might not care or want to help. But it's what I can do, for now."

"And while we wait?" Jessica asked.

"We just wait," he said. "You need to stay here, stay quiet. I'll bring you food."

She didn't like the sound of this. Stay here? Keep quiet? No, thank you. Just someone telling her she *had* to stay put made her want to run outside and dance around, shouting at the top of her lungs.

"I'm gonna get bored," she said, taking a drink from the

tequila bottle to wash down the sticky peanut butter in her mouth.

"I'll keep you company," Marcus said slowly.

"Such a hardship," she teased. She was...flirting with him. Why, she had no idea. She'd blame it on the tequila. Then she remembered something he'd said earlier. "Everyone else in here was put here because they couldn't behave, you said. So, why are you here? Specifically."

"Specifically, I'd say that's none of your business."

She sat back and folded her arms across her chest. So he'd talk about his missing hand, but not his very reason for being stuck in this place? Whatever. "Okay, you don't want to talk about it. I get it. Then tell me something else."

"Look, Jennifer. The less you know about me, the better."

"Look, Manford. The less you tell me, the more I'm gonna pry."

His face shuttered, all expression leaving it. Then he shoved the rest of his sandwich in his mouth, stood up, and left the trailer.

Jessica watched him go, shocked into silence. The man was moodier than a fourteen-year-old.

8

I t wasn't just Jessica's question that had sent Marcus running—it was her scent, her smile, her curves. It didn't matter that she was in the Junkyard against her will, by a total accident. He wanted her.

And fuck if that didn't make him an even worse person than he'd felt before.

A helpless human woman was trapped in the Junkyard and he was no better than the other pricks in here, half-hard all the time just from the sweet floral scent that rose from her skin like some kind of drug.

This all-encompassing desire was going to be the death of him, he was sure of it.

He took deep breaths of the clean forest air. Pine and fir trees surrounded him, and loamy, dusty scents of the earth rose up to meet his nose. Dappled moonlight stretched through the trees, highlighting pine cones, lichen-covered rocks, and little tufts of brilliant green grasses. There was beauty all around, but none of it compared with the beautiful woman he'd left in the camp trailer.

Soft footsteps met his ears, but he didn't turn around to

see her leaving the trailer. Her presence both soothed his inner wolf and riled it up at the same time.

"I'm not a safe person to be around," he said into the darkness.

"I'm not afraid of you," she said, touching his arm where his wrist ended, where his right hand used to be.

This place on his body had signaled his failure to protect Lena, and his failure as a fighter. And Jessica's gentle touch there nearly knocked him to his knees.

"You should be afraid," he said. "I'm no good for you."

She laughed quietly. "Maybe I'm too drunk to be afraid."

"Too pretty to be afraid." What was in that tequila, some kind of truth serum? He should shut up. Now.

"Aw, you think I'm pretty?" she asked.

Unable to resist looking down at her, he turned his head to take her in. Dark curls fell around her shoulders. Her full lips quirked up on one side in a half-smile, and her deep brown eyes arrested him, holding him in place.

He clenched his teeth together. He shouldn't say anything. He could be quiet as anything if he wanted to. He didn't need to say a motherfucking word— "You're prettier than pretty, Jessica."

She made a little sound in her throat. He couldn't tell whether it meant doubt, or approval, or what.

He felt her hand on his cheek next, and he closed his eyes. Simply being touched...it had been so long.

Turning his head, he pressed his mouth against her palm. And heaven help him, he couldn't resist pursing his lips and leaving a gentle kiss there before pulling back.

Even though he was afraid to see how she reacted, he opened his eyes. Her lips were parted slightly, and that freesia scent she carried surrounded him, winding around him like a spell.

"I need to take you in my arms," he said, his voice hoarse. "I need to kiss you."

She was quiet for a long moment, and he feared he'd messed everything up.

"I'd like that," she finally whispered.

He pulled her to him, and his heart pounded triple-time in his chest, a rhythm of need. Her hair was soft under his hand, and he wound the strands through his fingers before gripping the back of her neck. She gave a soft cry of surprise as he held her head exactly where he wanted it and pressed his mouth to hers.

Her lips were soft, sweet, and they readily opened for him when he swiped his tongue against them for a taste. She moaned softly into his mouth and held tight to his shoulders.

His cock ached, heavy and hard between them, and he fought the urge to rub himself against her soft lower belly. She seemed to have no such reservations, though, because she hooked one of her legs around his and pressed her body closer.

He twined his tongue with hers, picking up notes of tequila. Her scent was everywhere—not just the flowery freesia this time, but her desire. Heady. Sweet. He wanted to tear off her clothes, bury his face between her thighs and taste everything she had to offer.

What was he thinking? This thing between them was temporary at best, and the only thing *he* had to offer was a whole world of violence and heartache.

Reluctantly, he pulled back. She tried to follow him, but he kept his grip on her neck and eased farther away.

Her brown eyes were wide in question.

"This is a bad idea," he said, releasing her neck. "We can't do this."

"The hell we can't." She grabbed his t-shirt and tugged him forward again.

He allowed the kiss—the passion and anger she fueled it with were like a drug to his inner wolf. But when she reached for the waistband of his jeans, he grabbed her wrist and held her fast.

"We can't," he repeated. "Go to sleep, Jessica."

Hurt flashed over her face before she nodded. Her gaze went hard. "Of course. Drunken mistake. It won't happen again."

His inner wolf howled at the thought that this couldn't happen again, but she was right.

He waited until she was safely in the camp trailer. The latch bolted into place, and he ran to his cabin as fast as he could. Any slower, and the wolf would win, and he'd go back to that trailer and knock down the damn door in his eagerness to get to Jessica.

9

L eaning against the camp trailer door, Jessica took deep breaths.

"A drunken mistake," she had told him. Typical Jessica, lashing out when she felt rejected. Her parents had incited that behavior in her, too, even when she was little.

She remembered her dad looking debonair and stiff in his tuxedo, his dark beard well-trimmed, his glasses catching the light from the chandelier in their entryway.

"Can I come? Please? Please let me come this time," Jessica had said as a six-year-old, twirling in her favorite nightgown. She'd liked it because it was covered in a pattern of flowering vines. Surely it was pretty enough for a fancy party.

He'd given her a pat on the head and said, "No, Jessie, you can't come to Mommy and Daddy's book party. Maybe some other time."

It was the same answer he always gave. She had learned to hate it every time they finished a new book, because it meant more parties she couldn't go to.

"Fine! I didn't wanna go anyway. I hate your stupid books."

"Don't act spoiled, Jessie," her mom would say.

And then her parents would float out the door anyway, looking glamorous and leaving Jessica with yet another babysitter. They'd been completely unaffected by her words.

But Marcus? Marcus had been affected.

His nostrils had flared. Anger? Suspicion? He'd said he could tell when someone was lying. Did that mean he knew, right now, that there was a big part of Jessica's heart yelling *not a mistake*?

She reached behind her head and touched the back of her neck where he'd so carefully held her in place. His fingers had been almost bruising, yet she'd liked the pressure. It had signaled he was barely in control.

She'd driven him crazy with desire, and she liked it.

But seriously, what the hell had she been thinking? She didn't know this guy, not really.

She had *never* come on to one of the guys her parents were always trying to set her up with. Maybe because they'd worn neatly pressed shirts—ironed, no doubt, by a maid—and their hands were soft, like they'd never touched anything rougher than polished silver spoons and cashmere.

Her brain bounced back and forth between reassuring herself that she and Marcus shouldn't touch at all, and telling her to run out there and make him touch her everywhere.

"This is a bad idea," he'd said. "I'm no good for you."

But he hadn't said why.

She flopped down on the tiny bed at the end of the trailer and stared at the ceiling. The blankets still smelled like him. She liked his earthy, manly scent.

But if he was going to insist on acting like a butt smear, she could keep her distance. Fine. It was probably better this way.

And maybe she could find some other way out of this place. Maybe she didn't need his help after all.

SHE DREAMED she was trapped in a clear glass box. Her eyes were open, but her body was paralyzed, unable to move. A parade of animals walked around the glass box in laps, and she could only see them from her peripheral vision. A panther, a tiger, a bear, and a wolf, among others. Then the wolf stood on its hind legs. It lifted the box's lid. A fresh breeze blew over Jessica's skin, chilling her, but she was unable to move.

The wolf gazed down at Jessica with beautiful gray eyes. His fur disappeared, revealing human skin and a human form—it was Marcus. He bent forward and kissed Jessica.

His lips sent a tingling sensation through her body, awakening her nerves. Sitting up, Jessica looked around. The other animals were gone, and only Marcus remained. He took her hand, and the two of them walked into the woods together.

"What are we doing?" she asked.

He merely smiled, then let go of her hand. He reached behind her neck, beneath her hair, and gripped her in the same way he had outside the trailer—commanding, possessive. When he brought his lips to hers, the heat between them grew and grew.

"I want you," Jessica said.

"Good. I want you, too." He lowered himself to the ground and guided her down so she straddled his lap.

They were both naked. She hadn't really noticed that before. He cupped her face in his hand and against his wrist. His gray gaze was penetrating, like he was staring into her heart and learning everything about her. She did the same, staring back at him and feeling as if she knew him, feeling as if she'd known him for the entirety of her existence on this earth.

"You're mine," he said.

"Yes."

"I want you always," he said. "Do you want me?"

Leaning forward, Jessica kissed him. "Yes."

"You're mine," he said a second time, and then he lifted her off his thighs and lowered her onto his cock.

Jessica woke with a gasp. The trailer was dark, and she had no guess as to what time it was. Her stupid phone dying had left her feeling untethered and unsure, even if it had been useless for wifi or calls before it died.

The threads of her dream taunted her. She tried clinging to the mental wisps, but they floated out of reach. Only one part remained with her, a deep voice—Marcus's?—growling out the words *you're mine*.

If it had been Marcus in her dream, then it was all wrong. He'd all but shoved her away from him in real life.

Swinging her legs over the edge of the bed, she stood. She told herself she didn't need Marcus and she didn't want him, anyway.

What she really wanted was to talk to Blythe.

Marcus had told her it was dangerous. But now, the woods were silent. Everyone would be sleeping.

Jessica found her sneakers and slid them on. Carefully, she eased open the trailer door.

All was quiet outside.

She had no idea where Blythe was. While she knew this

was in some ways a fool's errand, Jessica couldn't resist at least trying to find Blythe.

Evaluating the darkness outside, she decided that she would walk for half an hour, tops, and she'd follow that gravel line so she wouldn't get lost. At the first hint of anyone around, she'd run back to the trailer and lock herself inside.

Marcus, AKA Mr. Bossypants, would never need to know she'd left.

10

When Marcus woke, it was still dark. There was no sound. He lay with his eyes open, staring at the planks of the cabin's ceiling, wondering what could have woken him.

The only thing he could discern was a distinct tugging sensation in his gut.

It didn't take him long to guess what caused the sense of unease. Jessica. Something was wrong, although he didn't know what.

He clambered out of bed and pulled on his jeans, then some socks and shoes. He grabbed a shirt on his way out the door.

Once outside, he gazed around him. The Junkyard was quiet save for a slight breeze blowing through the tree branches, rustling leaves. Something thudded to the ground nearby and he growled while zeroing in on it.

A pine cone. A fuckin' pine cone.

This sensation of *wrongness* was messing with his head and his reflexes.

He took off at a jog toward the trailer. Something was

wrong; he could feel it in his chest, in his gut. Was Jessica in danger? He'd never forgive himself if something happened to her. He knew he should've stayed the night in the trailer. He'd just been so fucking scared about taking advantage of her.

He hadn't wanted to risk it.

Story of his life. He took all the wrong risks and held himself back from the right ones.

When the trailer, with its painted murals, came into view, he sped his pace and called out, "Jessica?"

No answer. He skidded to a halt next to the door and yanked it open, not caring about her privacy—safety was more important and he could ask her to forgive him later if he offended her.

The trailer was empty.

Heart in his throat, he sniffed around outside the door. She'd gone east along the gravel line, so he went that way, too. Thankfully, it wasn't in the direction of any of the other shifters—this was the far side of the Junkyard from the dump.

Using his nose as his guide, he followed the boundary. After he'd walked a few yards, he saw her. She strode forward with purpose, like she was on a mission, her hair loose around her shoulders and waving behind her with each long stride.

"Jessica," he called.

She turned around, flipped him off, then turned again and continued on her way.

No longer panicked at her absence, he laughed. It was part relief, part exasperation. He couldn't sense anyone else nearby, although if she kept walking, eventually she'd reach the dump and all the shifters who lived around it.

"Hey, stop," he said.

She shook her head and grumbled something to herself. It sounded like "bossy pants butt smear," but that couldn't be right, could it?

Walking faster after her, he said, "If you don't come back to the trailer right the fuck now, I will throw you over my shoulder and carry you there."

"Ha," she said, kicking a pine cone from her path. "I dare you to try."

His inner wolf liked the challenge in her voice, the feistiness. He caught up with her in two seconds and she gave a little squeak when he gathered her in his arms and lifted her over his shoulder.

"What—the hell—are you doing?" she gasped.

"You dared me to try throwing you over my shoulder to take you back to the trailer. So here I am."

"I have never met a person more aggravating than you, Martin," she spat.

"Yes, well, the feeling's mutual, Jezebel," he grumbled, resting his hand on her backside to keep her from squirming free. He rather liked her slung over his shoulder like this.

"You are a terrible, awful man. And when I get free, I'm going to pick *you* up and...and then I'll throw you in the lake."

He abruptly switched course. "The lake. That's a great idea."

"Wait, what? No!"

She spun around awkwardly to get a view of where he was taking them.

"Can you swim?" he asked.

"No. I sink like a stone."

It was a lie, and he laughed.

"Marcus, I was just kidding," she said desperately. "I'd

never throw you in the lake. I wouldn't even be able to, remember? Frail human woman, no muscles, no speed. How could I even try? Besides, I like you. You're really quite nice and your ass is tight. I bet you could bounce a quarter off it. Maybe we should try that, right now? I think there's a quarter in my backpack."

The lake was in view and her scrambling—and panicked reasoning—increased. He grinned to himself. This was the most fun he'd had in...well, since he could remember.

"Marcus," she said sweetly, "I'll be your best friend..."

He waded into the water, not caring about his shoes and jeans getting wet. They'd dry later today in the afternoon heat.

"I make a great friend," she said. "I still have half a bottle of tequila. I'll give it to you, because you're my new best friend."

"I'm not interested in your tequila," he said.

"Then what are you interested in?"

He wasn't about to answer that question, because what he was interested in was her naked body, writhing beneath his, her beautiful lips parted while she was in the throes of an orgasm.

Once he was in water up to his thighs, he stopped.

"Marcus, don't do this, I swear, I'll—"

Her words ended in a shriek as she flew through the air and landed in the water.

She came up sputtering and wiping wet strands of hair out of her face. Her shirt clung to her curves, revealing the lacy pattern on her bra.

"I will end you!" she shouted, splashing him.

Arms crossed over his chest, he watched in amusement as she waded over to him. Then he saw she was shivering.

"Oh, hell," he said, reaching for her.

She tried to dodge him, but she slipped and fell with a screech. He hauled her out of the water and tugged her close, warming her as much as he could with his arms. He'd forgotten that humans weren't as tolerant to the cold as shifters.

"Come on, let's dry you off," he said.

Her teeth were chattering and he felt like the world's biggest asshole. Thankfully it was summer and the lake wasn't as cold as usual. But it was also still dark outside and the sun hadn't had a chance to warm the water.

He led her to the shore, arm around her shaking shoulders. He let her go so he could peel off his shirt, which was only slightly damp. When he started to drape it over her, he realized that it wouldn't do any good because of her wet clothes.

"Can you take off your shirt?" he asked. "I'll turn around so you have some privacy. Then you can put mine on."

"O-o-okay," she said, still shivering.

He turned while she changed shirts. Once she was done, he tugged her into his arms again. "I'm sorry, I didn't think about how cold it would be for you. Come on, let's go back to the trailer."

She walked with him, rubbing her hands over her arms as they went. He wanted to pick her up and carry her again, but he was afraid she was mad about the lake, and maybe he should keep his hands to himself as much as possible.

The sun would be rising soon. Already, birds were waking up in the faint pre-dawn light. He could hear other critters stirring, as well.

They reached the trailer. She pointed at it. "I never had a chance to ask you, yesterday, who did the paintings?"

"A guy named Grant. He lives over there." Marcus

gestured to the cabin. Encouraged that she was talking to him, he said, "I really am sorry about the cold water."

She flashed him a little smile. "It's okay. Next time *I'm* throwing *you*."

"You can try." Hell, he'd jump in with her, and he might've done so this morning except she'd been so cold.

He opened the trailer door and she went in.

"Two seconds," she said. "I just need to change out of my jeans."

Groaning to himself at the delightfully forbidden thought of her naked legs, he leaned against the side of the trailer. The morning sun was finally breaking through the trees and birds were beginning their chorus in earnest. The day would be hot, if the already rising temperature was any indication. He was glad, if for no other reason than it would help Jessica warm up faster.

"Idiot," he muttered to himself. His shoes were soaked, but he decided to leave them on. They'd dry eventually.

The trailer door opened and she stepped out. She was still wearing his shirt, and it draped over her, so long it almost reached the hem of her jean shorts.

He looked her up and down, relieved to see she was no longer shivering. "You're okay?" he asked.

"Yeah," she grumbled. "No thanks to you."

"I told you it's dangerous out there."

"I wanted to see Blythe," she said in a quiet voice.

He took a deep breath, wishing for patience. "Sometimes what we want is not what we can get."

"Obviously," she said in a strange tone of voice.

Why was she looking at him like that? Her brown eyes seemed to communicate something more than her words.

"Look, if you'd just stay put, you'd be fine," he said. Why couldn't she understand this very basic principle?

"Fine, but not *free*." She folded her arms over her chest, and the motion pushed up her tits, which were heaving from her angry breathing.

She looked amazing in his t-shirt.

"True," he said. "But nobody's free in the Junkyard. The most we're hoping for right now is safe. If you're safe, there's hope of getting you out, and then you can be as free as your cute little ass desires. Okay?"

Shaking her head, she said, "How do you do that?"

"Do what?"

"Say something that pisses me off, in such a sexy way."

He laughed—he couldn't help it.

"There you go again," she said. "Pissing me off."

"C'mere, Jessica."

Her eyes widened. He could easily get lost in those chocolate depths. She took one step toward him, then another.

"You look so pretty in my shirt," he whispered, reaching forward to touch the edge of the collar where it met her skin.

"I—" She didn't finish the sentence, her breath hitching.

"You what?"

"I...I don't know."

"Tell me you don't want me to touch you." He couldn't keep the raw need from his voice.

Her eyes flashed, and she placed one of her hands over his, holding it against her neck and bringing it to her nape, where he'd gripped her yesterday. She took his other arm and brought it to her waist. "I want you to touch me, Marcus."

Whatever she wanted, he would give her. Even if it wasn't good for her in the end.

He was just selfish enough for that.

11

M arcus's kiss was soft. It asked permission, much the way he had with his words. And when she gave permission, opening her mouth to him and allowing the kiss to deepen, he took more. His tongue dipped into her mouth, warm and sensuous. He tasted like the woods, sharp and clean. When he gently pulled back so they could breathe, Jessica couldn't help her whimper of dismay.

"More?" he asked, his voice gruff.

"Yes. More."

This time he squeezed the back of her neck, holding her in place so he could ravage her mouth. She gasped into the kiss and curled her hands around his shoulders. This kiss—his mouth, his lips—short-circuited her brain. Thinking was impossible. All was sensation. Taste—fresh forest. Scent—moss and male musk. Touch—the rough hairs on his arms, the firm press of his lips against hers. Sound—their heavy breathing, the pounding of her heart.

She couldn't remember ever wanting a man like she wanted Marcus. His muscles rippled beneath her touch, his lips moved against her mouth in a command. He adjusted his grip on her neck, tilting her head back, and trailed kisses down her throat. She shivered, not because she was cold, but because her body didn't know how to handle all of this pleasure.

He let go of her neck to slide his hand down between her breasts over the shirt. When he reached the hem, he paused.

"Yes," Jessica whispered. "Take it off."

She felt his lips moving as he grinned against the hollow of her throat.

"You're eager, aren't you?"

"Have you seen you?" she asked. "Of course I'm eager. Ravish me, muscle man."

"Gladly."

He left the shirt on her, but unfastened her jean shorts. When his hot fingers dipped below the waistband of her panties, she couldn't help the wanton moan that escaped her throat. Yes—this would ease the tension that had been building between them for two days.

"I'm going to take care of you," he whispered against her neck before nipping her ear, then licking away the sting.

"Yes," she said.

He slid his fingers against her folds, which were already slick with her arousal. "You're going to come on my fingers, Jessica. Do you want to come?"

"Yes." Her entire body felt alight with need. His dirty talk was doing it for her. That, and his scorching touch and wicked kisses.

He pressed one finger inside of her and she clenched around him, squeezing and rocking her hips back and forth to get friction from the heel of his hand against her clit. She couldn't think, couldn't speak—she could only move, lost in her need of his touch.

"You're squeezing me so tight," Marcus whispered, rubbing his scratchy whiskers against her neck. "Fuck, Jessica. You feel so good."

The low rumble of his voice and the slide of his fingers combined with the sting of his teeth and whiskers catapulted her into heights she hadn't thought possible. She cried out and he continued pumping his finger inside of her, drawing more pleasure from her while she came down from the high.

He leaned back slightly and pulled his hand from her panties.

Then he licked his fingers.

She couldn't take her eyes off of him, off the way his tongue lapped up her arousal.

"That was the hottest thing I've ever done," he said, his gray eyes dark with lust.

"We can do it again," Jessica breathed. "Anytime."

Hell, they could do it again right now. She wanted more than his fingers, though.

"Trust me, I want nothing more than to do that over and over with you." His eyes were intense, holding her in place just as effectively as his muscular arms. "But—"

"But it's not a good idea," she said, disappointment flooding her heart.

He sighed. "Yeah. I'm no good for you."

That old story. Again. It was feeling like one of those repetitive narratives her mom was always complaining that her dad would try to put into their plot outlines.

She shook her head, fighting the pain of rejection through the bliss of satisfaction running through her body.

"I should go," he said.

"Yeah. Okay." She didn't know what else there was to say about it. He'd made his feelings clear—more than once.

He walked away, his jeans darker on the bottom, wet from his walk into the lake. His stride was slow and purposeful, his shoulders down. She could see the regret in his posture until he was out of sight.

What was with this guy? She wanted him, he wanted her. Seemed easy enough for them to each take what they wanted. Second-guessing their desires at every turn was only serving to frustrate them both.

Her jean shorts were still unbuttoned and unzipped, so she reached down and hurriedly fastened them. She would not cry, she would not be embarrassed, she would not admit to herself that this guy did it for her.

But he elicited feelings in her that she'd never had before, for anyone.

Her parents had paraded dozens of well-to-do, "nice," eligible young men through their house. And all she wanted was Marcus.

But if he couldn't admit to himself what *he* wanted, then she wasn't going to waste her time on him anymore.

Even if it broke her heart.

She went into the trailer and made herself a peanut butter and apple sandwich. It stuck to her throat, and the pain of swallowing was what caused her eyes to water, nothing else. Certainly not a strong, handsome man with gorgeous gray eyes who'd rocked her world and left her heartbroken afterward.

Two taps on the side of the trailer made Jessica perk up. Had he seen some sense and come back? Another tap hit the trailer. It didn't sound like a knock, more like a pebble or something. She slid the dingy curtains aside from the slatted jalousie window and peeked outside.

A blond woman stood at the gravel line. She waved when she saw Jessica looking at her.

Jessica set down the remains of her sandwich and hurried out the door.

"Hi," the woman said. She had on khaki shorts and a light green tank top. "I'm Caitlyn. I'm part of the informal welcoming committee."

Her wry smile showed humor, and it was clear that Caitlyn knew Jessica was trapped in here.

Jessica smiled. "Hey, I'm Jessica. New resident."

"Do you need anything?" Caitlyn asked, pointing at the cabin behind her. "I have some extra food, and I could bring you clothes, tampons, whatever you might need."

"I'm okay for now, thanks," Jessica said. "Hoping to get out of here soon, and I came in with a full backpack."

"Oh, nice." Caitlyn hesitated at the gravel line, running the toe of her sandal along it. "Marcus probably told you that we're trying to track down a witch to help you out."

"Yes, I appreciate that," Jessica said. "My friend and I need to get out of here. What is this place, really? Marcus said it's like a prison for shapeshifters." She gave a little laugh, because seriously. Shapeshifters?

Caitlyn didn't laugh. She didn't even crack a smile. "He's telling you the truth."

"He's—no." Jessica shook her head.

Had everyone in this area lost their flipping minds? Then again, she was trapped in her by an invisible wall and she was waiting for a witch to free her, so...maybe the whole shapeshifter thing really wasn't all that extraordinary.

"I know it can be hard in there," Caitlyn said in a gentle voice. "But some of the guys are really great. Marcus is one of the good ones."

Marcus was amazing.

And Marcus could maybe turn into an animal.

She tried to wrap her head around the idea, but it was preposterous.

"It's a lot, I know," Caitlyn said. "I didn't know anything about shifters when I got stuck in there, either."

"You got stuck in here?"

"Yeah."

"Were you wandering around in the dark, drunk off tequila?" Jessica asked.

The corner of Caitlyn's lips twitched, then she laughed. "Sorry, sorry, I shouldn't be laughing. It's really not funny."

Jessica shrugged and let herself smile. "Really, it kind of is. I mean, except for everything else."

"Some of the other guys tricked me into crossing the line," Caitlyn said, sobering from her laughter. "Alleman purposefully injured himself so I went in to help. Then Mathers grabbed me."

"Wow." Jessica's chest tightened with dread, her body reacting to Caitlyn's story. "That's terrible."

"It was."

"But...you're not in here now," Jessica said. "Obviously."

"No, we were able to get out."

"Did you contact the witch?"

"We did—"

"Caitlyn," a man called from the cabin. "Your boss is on the phone."

"Oh!" Caitlyn gave Jessica an apologetic smile. "Sorry, I forgot I had a telephone meeting scheduled. We'll talk later? And let me know if you need anything. Just give a shout."

"Okay, thank you," Jessica said.

Caitlyn gave her a little wave and then jogged over to the little cabin.

So it *was* possible to get out of here. The witch had

helped Caitlyn, so the chances were high she would also help Jessica and Blythe.

Comforting herself with that notion, Jessica started toward the trailer to try to find something, anything to do. She got sidetracked by a damp area of earth near some fir trees. A different variety of plants grew around it—it must have been a spring, but it didn't lead anywhere. She mentally surveyed her discoveries.

There was a bright side to everything, and Jessica had just found the bright side to this strange turn her life had taken.

Here, she could look at plants to her heart's content, and she wasn't struggling to write a chapter that Chaole wouldn't hate.

12

Marcus spent the day walking the woods between his cabin and the camp trailer. Jessica's scent clung to him. The sighing of the breeze through tree branches reminded him of the way she'd sighed when he held her. He couldn't get the image of her brown eyes locked on his out of his mind.

He had hated—*hated*—leaving her side.

Throughout the rest of the morning, he prowled in circuits, making sure no other shifters were interested in the camp trailer. No one approached, and he mostly heard shouts and cheers from the direction of the dump.

If people were distracted with fighting, maybe now would be a good time to sneak in and snag one of those crystals Grant had mentioned.

On his next loop toward the western side of the Junkyard, Marcus didn't turn around at the pond. Instead, he kept going until he reached the scattering of rusted vehicles and other mechanical detritus. Just past them was the old quarry. He sniffed the air. This was Derrick Alleman's area. Damien Buenevista lived around here, too, and Stetson

Krom. Alleman was not a good guy. Buenevista—Marcus had no idea, as he'd barely seen the guy more than a couple of times. And Stetson? He was all right. Didn't talk much. Read a lot of books, or pretended to, at least.

None of them seemed to be around, so Marcus darted forward.

"What are you doing here, One-hand?" a voice called.

Shit. Marcus kept his stance casual as he looked over his shoulder at the mountain lion shifter who leaned against a stack of flattened cars. Derrick Alleman—the last guy he wanted to see.

"Just wanted to look at the quarry," Marcus said. "Maybe pick up a rock or two."

"It's rude to run through my back yard."

Marcus kept his retort to himself. This was hardly a back yard. It was a dump in both name and appearance. He could even see plastic food wrappers half-buried in the ground. Everyone else bagged up their trash to send out when new food came in, or buried their compostable garbage. Alleman was a slob, letting his den look like this.

Marcus kicked at a half-empty jar of jelly, the remaining contents rotten inside, coated in mold. "Sorry about that. I figured you'd be at the fights with everyone else. Didn't want to disturb you."

Alleman stood up straighter. "You joining the fights, Bylund? You seemed intent on that pretty redhead a couple nights ago."

"I don't think so." Marcus started forward.

"Nah, seriously, man. If you don't think it'll be fair, I'll fight you with a hand tied behind my back." He chortled at the idea. "Get it?"

"Yeah, you're a real comedian," Marcus said.

"Don't fuck with me. Why are you going to the quarry?"

"I want a rock."

Alleman scratched his stomach. "Whatever. Maybe the rock'll keep you company while the redhead warms my dick."

"You're not going to win," Marcus said.

"The hell I'm not."

A roar of pain rose up from the center of the dump, and Alleman raised his eyebrows.

"Everyone's training," Alleman said. "The big fight'll be in two weeks. You want a chance at pussy, you better join in."

"Yeah, okay." Inside, his gut churned. Jessica's friend was okay for now, but how long would she stay that way? Once the fight took place, he doubted the Junkyard shifters would let something like Blythe's metal pipe keep them at bay. They'd work together to help the winner claim his prize.

Alleman gave Marcus a hard look, then turned and wandered in the direction of the fighting.

Marcus hurried forward, not wanting to run into anyone else.

The quarry was a dusty indentation in the earth that collected rainwater if the clouds emptied enough. Clear, white crystals dotted the rubble. Marcus quickly grabbed one of them and stuffed it into his pocket. It didn't seem so special to him. But he wasn't a witch, so what did he know? He'd take a closer look at it later, maybe, but right now he was feeling antsy after leaving Jessica for so long. He hadn't planned on the interrogation from Alleman. Too much time had passed, and he'd feel better once he could resume his patrol around the camp trailer.

Thunderclouds rolled overhead, and the wind picked up. Another mountain thunderstorm would start soon, maybe in a few hours. Marcus actually liked them, although the rumblings from the heavens caused a pang when he remembered how Marianne would only allow Marcus to be the one to comfort her during storms. Their mom couldn't do the trick, nor her dad. She'd said only her wolf brother could help.

He wondered whether his wolf nature seemed tougher to her, or whether she'd simply believed it took a monster to defeat a monster.

The trailer came into view, and just in front of it, Jessica was pacing. She started when she saw Marcus, then she scowled and turned away. She darted around the other side of it. A second later, he heard the trailer door slamming shut.

Well, he hadn't expected the warmest of welcomes after the way he'd left her this morning, but he also hadn't expected to be so thoroughly dismissed.

"Jessica?" He took big steps to reach the trailer faster.

When he reached the door, he tried to tug it open.

It was locked.

"Dammit, Jessica, what's going on? Let me in, now."

Her voice was muffled through the door. "Or, what, you'll *blow my house down*?"

"Is this about the shifter thing?" he asked, taken aback.

The door opened, and Jessica stuck her head out. Her brown curls were in disarray and her brown eyes were narrowed in irritation.

"No, it's not about the quote unquote *shifter thing*. I don't want to talk to you, *Maximillian*," she said. "You come back here with your sexy swagger and your happy fingers and you expect me to just—to just *swoon*. Well, I'm not swooning."

He couldn't keep his smile from forming. She was too fuckin' cute.

"It's not a joke, Marshall." She frowned.

"Okay, okay." He wiped the smile off his face. "I'm sorry. Tell me what this is about."

"I just did. I don't like how you took off. And I've been alone for hours, with only one other person to talk to."

Alarm shot through him. "Wait—who did you talk to?"

"Caitlyn."

He exhaled.

She peered up at him. "I'm seriously going stir-crazy here, with no news, no connections to anyone else. Caitlyn was super nice, but she can't stand at the gravel line forever."

"No, she can't, and yes, you're right." He held out his hand. "Come here. I'll tell you where I was, and everything I just found out."

They walked to a weathered log and sat down. Jessica pulled up one of her legs and propped her chin on it while she listened to Marcus talk. He spent the next hour listing all the guys he knew in the Junkyard—Jase Englender, Stetson Krom, Noah Ephraimson, Damien Buenevista, Derrick Alleman, Ronan Markowicz, Fred Barnum, and Beau Mollin. There were a few others who he didn't know very well at all, but getting Jessica familiar with the rest was a good start.

"So the guys to avoid are Buenevista, Alleman, Barnum, and Mollin," Jessica said.

"You should avoid all the guys," Marcus said. "We're all in here for a reason."

Jessica pursed her lips. "Including you."

"Right," he said, hoping she wouldn't press him for details like she had last time. "I don't know any of them particularly well. Jase is a stand-up guy, I guess. But all this is just from what I know in here. I have no idea who they truly are."

She was quiet for a moment. "How they are in here is all we have to go on. And if they've been decent thus far, I think we'll have to assume that's their true nature. Sometimes you have to look past someone's reputation, to find who they truly are."

Marcus basked in the thoughtful, understanding tone that went along with her words. She wasn't just talking about giving those other guys a chance—she was talking about Marcus, too.

But she didn't know what he'd done. She didn't know everything.

She should know. He didn't want to talk about it, but before she got too attached to him, he should tell her the truth of it all.

Taking a deep breath, he said, "I killed someone. Someone in my own pack."

He could sense her heart rate speeding up, but she didn't jump away from him.

He went on, "I came here and felt it was deserved."

"Was it deserved?" Jessica asked quietly.

Marcus shrugged. "The man I killed—I'd known him for years. He was in my pack. Not all packs are tight-knit, but mine was. The bond between all of us was strong. He was like a brother to me."

She touched his arm, sympathy welling in her eyes. "Then I'm sure you didn't just lash out and kill him for no reason at all."

"You're right. I was protecting my sister, Marianne. He was scaring her, and stalking her. His behavior was escalating. But nobody else thought so. Maybe I was wrong, maybe I was overprotective." Even now, he cringed at the memory, at Vince's surprise when Marcus first told him to leave Marianne alone.

"You don't really think you were being overprotective, do you?" she asked.

"No. I guess I don't. Every instinct I had told me that he wasn't joking around like he said he was. Every instinct I had told me that he wasn't in control like he said he was. And Marianne—she was scared. And he thought that was fine."

Jessica's fingers were soft against his arm. "I wasn't there, but it sounds like you did the right thing."

"Maybe." He looked up to watch the gray clouds rolling overhead. The wind lashed at the trees, and it would start raining soon; he could smell the change in the air. "It got me thrown in here, but I don't have regrets, at least not about protecting Marianne. But I miss her. And since I lost my hand, I can't fight like I used to. It's fine because generally, nobody cares what I do or where I go."

"I care," Jessica whispered.

"Well, that's the other thing. This fight for your friend is going to happen soon."

"What will the outcome be?" Jessica asked. "Which of the guys has the best chance?"

He shrugged. "I don't know. But I was thinking...if I toss my hat in the ring, so to speak, maybe I can give one of the good guys a fighting chance. Hopefully Grant will find the witch and you and Blythe will get out of here before any of this is necessary. But just in case that doesn't happen, we should have a fallback plan."

"So all that shouting I heard earlier," she said, "that wasn't them fighting for Blythe, was it?"

"No. I ran into Alleman and he said they're training for the big fight. But honestly, when *aren't* they fighting here, is the better question?"

"Always practicing," Jessica mused.

"Yep."

She slugged him in the bicep. "Well, let's go, Rocky. Let's train you up."

He took in her earnest brown eyes and wide smile. "Seriously?"

"Seriously." She looked around the little clearing. "What else are we going to do—count chipmunks?"

He could think of a few things they could do, but those things all involved getting naked, so he nodded. "Fine, let's do this."

"All right, champ." She stood up and put her hands on her hips. "I'm your coach, and your first task is…"

He waited while she tapped a finger against her lips. She obviously didn't know the first thing about training a fighter, but he didn't care.

"Maybe we should spar," he suggested. "So you can get a measure of my abilities."

"Okay. You should take off your shirt, then. So it doesn't get all sweaty when I'm kicking your ass." She winked.

He laughed, and did as she asked, pulling the cotton over his head and dropping it on the log where they'd been sitting. He didn't know if she was trying to cheer him up on purpose or what, but there was something about this woman—she was full of joy, and jokes. He hadn't smiled this much in months.

She obviously knew nothing about fighting, so he took her through the four basic punches—the jab, the uppercut, the cross, and the hook. He showed her how to hold her fist, how to swing from the gut, not the shoulder.

The dark clouds finally broke into a light drizzle, but he and Jessica remained outside, exchanging slow-motion blows and practicing blocking each other. Rain fell lightly over them, making Jessica's skin shine and her dark hair curl.

Something switched as their clothes soaked through. Marcus could sense it like he'd sensed the approaching storm. Their bodies moved in this sparring dance, learning each other's movements, anticipating contact. His breath hitched as he realized he was appreciating Jessica's curves as much as he was appreciating her quick mind.

Jessica came after him in a rush, like she really hoped to surprise him. He blocked her without any trouble, but grabbed her shoulder and spun her around until her back was flush against his front.

She was breathing hard, and she gasped in surprise. "How'd you do that? I didn't even see you move."

"As a shifter, I'm stronger. Faster. My senses are better, too."

She lifted her foot, probably to stomp on his instep, but he moved out of the way and picked her up.

"Dammit, Muhammad," she said in an adorable growl. "Put me down."

He put her down, but he didn't lose contact with her. He kept his hand on her shoulder, and his other arm at her waist. She faced away from him, so he couldn't see her expression, but he could feel the speedy beating of her heart.

"Tired, Jasmine?" he asked.

He kept his tone light, but his body yearned to be close to her. Touching her this morning, helping her come apart, had been heaven, and he wanted to go back to that moment and do it again.

Before he could stroke his fingers along her shoulder and down to her hip, the sound of footfalls reached his ears, combined with the faint scent of mountain lion. He looked up with a growl, searching the forest around them. He relaxed when he saw it was just Grant.

"Marcus," Grant said.

Jessica gave a squeak of alarm, but Marcus reassured her. "He's a friend. That's Grant, Caitlyn's mate."

Grant nodded at Jessica. "Hello. I just wanted to check in with you on the witch. She's ill, and the coven won't allow me to talk to her or send a message."

"Shit," Marcus said.

"You'll keep trying, though, right?" Jessica asked.

Grant gave her a small smile. "Of course. I'll keep trying, and I'll keep reinforcing the fact that you're human and shouldn't be in there to begin with."

"Thank you," Jessica said.

She was a lot more generous with her gratitude than Marcus was feeling. The witch lead wasn't working, and Marcus wanted to yell with frustration. Still, he thanked Grant before Grant walked away.

Then he faced Jessica. "I'm sorry."

"It's not your fault," she said. "None of it is."

He gave her a careful look and saw goosebumps rising along her neck and collar. "Come on, let's get you dried off. It's late, anyway."

He wanted to hold her, chase away the cold and disappointment, but that wasn't his job. His job was to protect her until he could set her free.

13

J essica tossed and turned on the trailer bed. Across the room, Marcus lay on the other bed, which was formed by taking down the dining table and throwing cushions on top of it. Kind of genius, really. She'd never spent time in a camp trailer before. Her vacations had been to different countries, for the most part, and nice hotels during book and publishing conferences, where she'd spent most of her time in the hotel pool, being watched by a nanny.

She wasn't complaining and she would never complain about that weird, lonely childhood—she knew so many people had worse upbringings. Blythe, for example. Blythe hadn't provided any details, but Jessica could tell there was some past hurt. Jessica, at least, hadn't been physically or mentally harmed. She'd always had enough to eat, and her parents, although absent a lot of the time, had loved her in their own remote way.

The rain pattered away at the roof of the trailer, making her feel safe and warm. Or maybe that was just Marcus's presence a few feet away. She was oh-so-tempted to go to him, throw him on his back, and grind against him until they each found release, but he'd made it clear, more than once, that he wasn't available to her in that way.

Except for that moment in the morning, when he'd fingered her to oblivion. Her thighs clenched involuntarily as the memory rocked through her mind.

"You still awake?" Marcus asked.

His voice was a low rumble. Wow, how she loved the way he sounded. Tough, dangerous. He'd killed a man, but he'd done it to protect someone. She wasn't afraid of him. Instead, she was drawn to him. He was a protector. He held a sorrow inside that she yearned to soothe.

"Yeah," she said, sitting up and looking in his direction.

He sat up, too; she could see the dark outline of his hulky build against the lighter wall of the trailer.

"It's still raining," he said.

"Yep." She wondered where he was going with this.

He hesitated. "You're sad about not seeing Blythe, and I was thinking."

"Okay."

"The rain should hide your scent. If we're careful, I think I could get you to Blythe so you can see for yourself that she's doing all right."

Jessica swung her legs off the bed. Her bare feet hit the cool linoleum. "I'm in. Let's do it."

"Just like that?" he said, amusement in his voice. "You're not scared of the big, bad shifters?"

"Ha. I haven't seen any evidence they exist. You say you can turn into an animal...where's the proof?" Her heart pounded at the thought of challenging him like this.

"You don't want to see," he said. "Trust me."

"I trust you on a lot of things, but not that."

He grumbled something about stubbornness under his

breath, but she ignored him and pulled on a pair of jeans, figuring it was dark enough he wouldn't be able to see much. She yanked off her night shirt, too, thinking she'd wear another one for this outing in the rain. She wanted to keep her night shirt dry.

He cleared his throat.

"What?" Jessica asked.

"I can see in the dark."

"Crap!" She yanked her arms down over her breasts.

"I'm looking away now," he said.

"How magnanimous of you."

"You've no idea."

Her face felt hot, and yet she didn't know why she should feel embarrassed or shy after the man had put his hand in her panties earlier in the day. Maybe if she showed him her goodies, she'd get lucky and he'd do that again.

And again.

Groaning, she found her bra and a long-sleeved shirt and put them on, followed by her tennis shoes.

"Okay," she said, "I'm ready."

He opened the door and humid air from the summer mountain storm rushed in.

It was dark—as dark as it had been the night Jessica and Blythe had gotten lost. How long ago was that, anyway? Two nights ago? It seemed like weeks. She'd just met Marcus, and she hardly knew anything about him, but she felt she *knew* him anyway. It wasn't just the way he'd so expertly taken control of her body and her pleasure. It was more about how her heart felt about his heart. Weird.

She tried to set the thoughts aside and focus on putting one foot in front of the other without walking herself straight into a tree. Marcus kept his arm against her shoulder and she welcomed its warm weight and subtle guiding presence. If he could see in the dark—and she had no doubt he could—then they were probably moving much slower than he'd be able to go on his own. Yet he didn't complain, didn't give huffs of impatience, didn't make her feel like she was inept.

He hadn't said anything about being silent, but the idea was there between them. She wouldn't speak unless he spoke first. After his run-down of the different guys in this place, she knew just how worried he was for her safety.

At least it was raining, and her scent would be masked. It was hard to wrap her head around the idea that people could *smell* her, but in the scheme of her whole world understanding changing in three days, it wasn't that preposterous.

They came out of the trees, and the landscape around her took on a lighter cast. She could make out distinct shapes—large rocks? She squinted, unable to tell. As they got closer, she realized this was the "dump" portion of the Junkyard that Marcus had told her about. The big shapes weren't boulders, but old cars and pieces of large machinery. A few yards away from her and Marcus was a school bus, tilted slightly on uneven ground. Jessica shivered. Not only was it an eerie sight, but her shirt was soaked through and the chill was getting to her.

Marcus wrapped his arm around her and guided her forward through the hulking cars. It was like visiting an apocalyptic setting full of mechanical monsters. Headlights were eyes gleaming with malevolence. Broken windshields were jagged teeth jutting up from gaping mouths.

"Here," he whispered, bringing her close to an RV on the other side of something that might have been a tractor in a previous life. "This is where she's staying."

She could make out the RV's striped panels, and an open window.

"Better you talk to her than me," Marcus said in a quiet voice.

Jessica nodded. Knocking against the side of the RV, she said, "Blythe? Are you awake?"

There was no answer, but she knocked again. "Hey, Blythe. It's Jessica."

Blythe's face appeared in the window, her pale skin making it easier for Jessica to see her.

"Jessica," Blythe whispered. "You're okay?"

Relief flooded Jessica at the sight of her friend's concerned face. If Blythe was concerned about Jessica's well-being, it meant Blythe was doing all right. "Yeah. This is... this is wild, though, right?"

Blythe nodded.

"Tell me about you," Jessica said. "Do you want to come out of there? You can stay with me."

Marcus cleared his throat and said, "I don't think that would be wise."

"We'd make it work," Jessica began. Why was he always saying things weren't safe or smart?

"They'd search for Blythe," Marcus explained, "and then they'd find you, too."

Blythe turned her attention to Marcus, and she scowled. "I was just going to say that." She turned back to Jessica. "I'm safe for now."

Jessica supposed it made sense. But she didn't have to like it.

She looked carefully at Blythe's face, searching for signs of abuse or malnourishment. "Marcus said some guy is bringing you food."

"Yeah, Jase. He's not as big of a dickhead as some of the

others."

"High praise," Jessica said with a little laugh.

"How about you?" Blythe asked. "What are you doing with that old man?"

"Old?" Jessica looked at Marcus in a new light. She supposed he was older than she and Blythe were, maybe mid-thirties.

Marcus grinned when he noticed her attention on him. "I'm thirty-nine."

"See?" Jessica said, looking back at Blythe. "Not that old. Not that it matters."

Blythe's eyebrows rose. "However old he is, it looks like he's taking care of you."

"Yeah, he is." Jessica couldn't keep the fondness from her voice.

Blythe's eyebrows rose and she opened her mouth to say something, but Marcus said, "Shh," and pressed Jessica down before grabbing her hand and dragging her around the RV to huddle between the RV's corner and the wheel well of the tractor next to it.

A man walked by, his eyes on the ground. He swayed slightly, like he was drunk. A line of blood spread from his nose down over his lips, but he didn't wipe it away. The rain smeared it to some extent.

Jessica held her breath. Her heart pounded faster than normal. She wanted to bolt into the darkness. If they stayed put, surely he would see her and Marcus crouched here by the RV. Only shadows protected them.

He tripped over something, maybe his own foot, but righted himself quickly, muttering, "Fuckers."

Then his gaze landed on the RV.

Jessica was afraid to exhale.

He sauntered over—thankfully to the other side of of the vehicle, opposite of where Jessica and Marcus hid.

"Hey, Red," he called. "Wanna come out and play?"

When Blythe didn't answer, he raised his voice. "Girlie. Come out and give Barnum some love."

The RV tilted toward Jessica and Marcus. He must have shoved it. Marcus yanked Jessica up onto the tractor quickly, so she wouldn't get squished between the RV and the tractor.

Blythe gave a little yelp, then shouted, "Try that again, asshole, and I'll smack you down!"

Another voice came from the darkness. "Barnum, go the fuck to sleep. Leave the woman alone."

"I'm horny," Barnum shouted back.

"Shut up and rub one out like everyone else has to do."

Jessica had to bite her lips to keep from giggling. A totally inappropriate reaction, but she couldn't help it.

Barnum groaned and shoved the RV again. As it rocked back into place, Marcus guided Jessica once again to the shadows between the tractor and RV. Just in time, as Barnum was coming around to walk past them.

His footsteps squelched in the mud and he tripped again, but he didn't fall. Jessica watched his retreating back as he continued on. Marcus's arm on her shoulder was a warm reassurance.

Long after Barnum was out of sight, Marcus said, "Okay. We need to go."

"Blythe?" Jessica said quietly through the nearest RV window. "I'll come again when I can."

"No, don't risk it," Blythe whispered back. "I'll be all right. This isn't the first time I've had to fight off monsters."

Jessica knew Blythe was trying to prove her toughness,

but the thought of her needing to fight for safety gave Jessica a pang of sorrow.

"Take care," Jessica whispered.

And then Marcus was pulling her by the hand—out of the shadows of the RV and over to the shadows of what looked like an old food truck. They hop-scotched through the dump from one clump of wreckage to another, although she noticed he gave a wide berth to one large structure. She guessed it was someone else's living quarters.

He froze next to the school bus, his hand tightening on Jessica's shoulder. She looked over at him in question. He lifted his arm to point up, and she realized—it had stopped raining.

He muttered a curse, then held out his arms. Jessica knew what he was offering without words, and she nodded. He picked her up, and then he ran with her to the trees. Jessica had to clench her jaw to keep her teeth from clacking together with each of his bouncing steps. There was no graceful way to ride in his arms like this, so she held on to his shoulder with one hand and wrapped her other arm around his neck.

Once they were in the shelter of the trees, Marcus slowed his pace. Jessica didn't have to hold on so tightly anymore, but she did anyway, because holding tight to him felt good.

All the way back to the trailer, he carried her. Their clothes were damp from the rain, but Jessica wasn't cold. Yet when they reached the trailer and he set her down so they could go inside, he didn't remain in contact like she wished. Instead, he waited for her to go inside and he hesitated in the doorway.

"Aren't you going to sleep here?" she asked.

"Maybe I should stay in my own cabin."

"Why?"

He made a face. "I'd rather not say. Short answer is I'm trying to be honorable."

A flash of irritation washed over her. Why was he resisting the pull between them? "Do you mean 'honorable' like you were this morning with your hand in my panties?"

"Fuck, Jessica. That's exactly it. I don't want to be a monster."

She folded her arms over her chest. The only monster she'd been aware of was the monster of an orgasm he'd given her.

But speaking of monsters, she wasn't sure she'd be able to fall asleep after nearly getting crushed by that guy in the dump.

Swallowing back the lump in her throat, she said, "Can you at least wait until I fall asleep?"

His eyes softened and he nodded. "Okay. Probably a good idea to stick around for a few minutes, make sure we weren't followed."

He sat on the far end of the trailer while she changed into her night shirt and took off her shoes, socks, and jeans. She faced the other way, but she hoped he was watching. She hoped he was tempted. The adrenaline she'd felt in the dump and on their rush back to the trailer was still coursing through her veins.

A low rumble filled the trailer, and as soon as her shirt was on, she spun around to look at him. "What was that?"

"Nothing." His voice was throaty, like the rumble.

"Were you...growling?"

"Maybe. Go to sleep, Jane."

Laughing to herself, she lay down and pulled the blanket over her legs. Then she stared up at the ceiling. Neither of them said anything for a full minute.

She couldn't sleep, not with questions and desire buzzing through her. So she said the first thing that popped into her mind.

"Why did you finger me earlier, if you don't want to mess around?"

"Let's talk about anything else," he said.

"Do you think it was a mistake?"

"Fuck no. Touching you could never be a mistake."

Huffing in exasperation, she said, "Then what is it?"

"I told you. I'm no good for you."

"Then be better." She turned onto her side and leaned up on an elbow so she could glare in his direction.

"I'm trying." He said it so quietly, she barely heard the words. Clearing his throat, he added, "What about you? What's your life like—what do you want to do?"

"I'm not sure," she said.

"That's not true."

"Damn you and your lie-sniffing." She sighed and lay back down, but she remained facing him. "I don't know what kind of *work* would go with this, but I really love plants."

"Like gardening?" he asked.

"No. I mean, I like that, too. But I like learning about different kinds of plants, what they do, how they interact with animals and each other. Some studies have shown that plants can recognize their siblings, and they compete less with them for resources than they would with unrelated plants."

"Wow," he said. "I had no idea."

"And there's a plant in the Philippines that can eat rats."

"Seriously?"

She grinned. "You didn't detect a lie in my voice, did you?"

His laughter was a low rumble. "No, I didn't. It's incredible. Rats, really?"

"Yep. *Nepenthes attenboroughii*. It's a pitcher plant."

"I don't know what that means."

"They're so cool. They have this sac thing, shaped like a pitcher. It's full of fluid that attracts insects—or, in the case of *Nepenthese attenboroughii*, rats. Then the fluid digests the prey."

He was quiet for a moment. "And you just know the scientific name, off the top of your head?"

"I don't know most scientific names," she admitted. "But I like the sound of this one, and it's named after David Attenborough—you know, the guy who narrates all those nature films?"

"No, I don't know him."

"Then you are missing out. When we get out of this place, that's the first thing we'll do—watch *Planet Earth*."

When he didn't say anything, she cleared her throat. "I *said*, we'll watch *Planet Earth*."

"Jessica. Nobody's going to let me out of the Junkyard. I'm not in here by mistake."

"Well, you don't deserve to be in here."

He didn't respond. She was getting tired of his broody silences. Then, finally, he whispered, "Goodnight, Jessica."

"Goodnight, Marcel." She flopped onto her back and stared at the ceiling until her heavy eyelids closed and sleep came.

14

The past three days had been some of the happiest in Marcus's life. Every morning, he left his cabin before the sun rose. Instead of roaming the lakeshore or the northern boundary of the Junkyard like he used to do, he loped toward Jessica's camp trailer.

Each day, they sparred, they talked, and they teased each other. Running through mock punches and kicks put them close physically, which he enjoyed. But he also liked the good-natured shit-talking that went along with it. He found himself making internal lists of names that started with J, so he'd always have a new one ready to call her. When she really wanted to tease Marcus, Jessica would come up with a ridiculous, deep voice and adopt what she called a "resting brood face."

There was laughter, there was touching. It was getting more and more difficult to keep from truly touching her, beyond what the sparring allowed. He'd had a taste, that one morning, of the sweetness she had to offer. He knew what she sounded like when she came. He'd felt the rhythmic pulsing of her pussy around his fingers, he'd felt her body shake with tremors afterward.

Yesterday had been the hardest and the best. She had leaped at him when he wasn't looking, and he'd gone down, falling on his ass. Falling was inevitable, with his center of balance out of whack because of her weight. But he'd slowed down the fall as much as possible so she wouldn't get hurt.

And where she'd landed? Straddling his waist, her hands on his shoulders.

They'd stared at each other for a long moment. The heat of her legs around his waist, against his cock, was a siren call.

He longed to sit up, grab the back of her neck, and kiss her senseless while she rubbed against him.

But then she'd abruptly scrambled off of his lap and crawled over to a blooming yellow flower.

"Look," she'd exclaimed, her brown eyes shining with excitement. "It's a Plumas rayless daisy!"

He'd squatted next to her. "What random fact do you know about this one?"

"No random facts," she said. "I just like them. I first saw them at the writing intensive and looked it up in one of the nature books they had in the dining hall. Look at their happy little blossoms."

"Yes, they look ecstatic," he agreed in a deadpan voice.

She tugged on his arm. "They are. I wonder what else is around that I didn't know about?"

Marcus hadn't had an answer for her, but the conversation had given him an idea. That night, after waiting until she fell asleep in her trailer, he'd found a mostly-blank notebook in his cabin, left there by Carter or a previous occupant. After tearing out the couple of pages with random scrawls on them, he spent the pre-dawn hours scouring the woods and clearings.

And now he was on his way to Stetson's den to see whether his idea was even possible.

For his den, Stetson had cobbled together an old van and added on something at the back with corrugated sheet metal and other scraps, including some car doors. Marcus had never taken a good look at the place; he'd never needed to, but he imagined Stetson had a spot inside where he kept all those books he pretended to read.

When Marcus approached, Stetson was sitting outside his den on an upside-down ice chest and leaning against the dusty blue exterior of the van, a book open in his hands and a cowboy hat pulled low over his forehead.

"You're really leaning into the whole *Stetson* thing, aren't you?" Marcus asked, gesturing at Stetson's hat.

"This ain't a Stetson hat," he responded. His voice was always scratchy, and Marcus wondered if it was because he didn't talk much.

Marcus could imagine Jessica's retort, *But it's Stetson's hat, get it?* And his lips twitched.

"What kinds of books do you have?" Marcus asked.

Stetson shrugged. "Whatever they bring me."

Holding his notebook tightly in the crook of his arm, Marcus said, "I'm looking for something about the plants in this area."

"Didn't take you for a naturalist," Stetson said.

Marcus wasn't going to lie to a shifter, so he kept quiet.

After tucking a piece of paper into his open book, Stetson closed it, stood up, and set it gently, almost reverently, on the overturned cooler. "I might have something about plants, don't know if it'll be for this area."

Marcus waited outside while Stetson opened the van

door and climbed inside. The van shifted slightly as Stetson moved around.

Stetson returned a couple of minutes later with three books in his hands. One was Michael Pollan's *The Botany of Desire*, one was *Leaves of Grass* by Walt Whitman, and the third was a guidebook of plants in the western U.S.

"Can I trade you something for these?" Marcus asked. He guessed Jessica would be most interested in the guidebook, but the other two couldn't hurt, with titles like those.

Stetson's gold eyes were evaluating. "Sure."

"What do you want? I could do some fishing for you."

"Already stole the catch you left by the lake last week."

Marcus had forgotten all about those. "My pole, too?"

"Yep." He reached into his den and pulled out Marcus's fishing pole.

"You can keep it," Marcus said. "For the books."

Nodding, Stetson said, "Deal."

Marcus nodded his thanks, tucked the books into the crook of his arm with the notebook, and headed northeast toward Jessica's trailer.

He was arriving later than usual, and he worried that she'd be anxious. But when he reached the trailer, she wasn't outside the rear of the trailer watching for him like she had been the past couple of days.

"Jessica?" he called softly.

No answer. She wouldn't have left again like she'd done before. He'd just checked in on Blythe yesterday morning and reported to Jessica that all was fine—Blythe was tired of being cooped up, but she was safe and still getting plenty to eat and drink; Jase was making sure of that.

He dropped the books and notebook on a flat rock and hurried around to the front of the trailer.

Jessica was sitting next to the gravel boundary, eating

breakfast with Caitlyn. It was Caitlyn who saw Marcus first, and she lifted her fork in a wave. Jessica turned around then, her brown eyes immediately locking with Marcus's.

He didn't know what it was—relief at finding her after worrying about her? Happiness because she made his heart feel lighter? Or the constant, pure, unadulterated desire urging him to possess her? Whatever the hell it was, it was impossible to ignore. He marched forward, held out his hand. When she grabbed it, he lifted her up and slanted his head toward hers, then took her mouth in a kiss so thorough it caused his inner wolf to howl in triumph.

Sweet maple syrup flavored her hot, wet mouth. All thoughts floated from his mind, replaced with the need to hold her and listen to her soft moans.

From her chair on the other side of the gravel line, Caitlyn whistled and clapped.

Marcus let go of Jessica and stared into her eyes. He didn't speak, but he was promising more. "Later," he said.

Jessica nodded at him, her chocolate eyes dilated and lust-drunk.

"Well," Caitlyn said, amusement in her voice. "I should probably get to work. If you want to pass your empty plate over, Jessica...?"

With her cheeks turning pink, Jessica said, "Yes, of course. Thank you so much for breakfast—it was delicious."

Jessica stepped away from Marcus so she could pass over her dishes. Caitlyn said goodbye with a smirk on her face and walked back to her cabin, picking her way through the long grasses that filled the clearing between the cabin and the trailer. Once she was out of sight, Jessica turned to Marcus.

"Mahatma, you wanna tell me what that kiss was about?"

"I hardly know." He shook his head. "My wolf wanted it. *I* wanted it. I'm tired of not kissing you. You're too hard to resist, Jacinda."

Jessica opened her mouth like she was going to say something, then closed it again.

"What is it?" Marcus asked.

She shook her head. "Let's just practice fighting stuff."

He looked at her. "Really. I want to know what you're thinking."

"Fine," she said, a stubborn tilt to her head. "Show me your wolf."

"My wolf," he said, his heart pounding.

"Yep. Caitlyn and I talked about all kinds of stuff—including what it's like being a human around shifters. I haven't seen anyone turn into an animal. I'm starting to believe shifters aren't really a thing. So, why don't you show me?"

Why didn't he show her? Because he didn't want to scare her off. She was human, he was a shifter. They were different, and he remembered her fear the night they'd met. She'd seen a wild animal and she'd been terrified.

"You're afraid," Jessica said.

"I'm scared of *you* being scared."

"Well, that's ridiculous." She folded her arms across her chest. "Don't underestimate me, Morpheus."

He took off his shirt and inwardly preened as her eyes got bigger.

"Three things," he said.

She nodded.

He went on, "First thing is, I'm still me when I'm the wolf. I hear you, I understand you."

"Okay. That's what Caitlyn said."

"The second thing is, I don't look like a fluffy pet dog. I look like a wolf. It might be frightening."

"I'm not scared."

He started working on the buttons of his jeans.

"What are you doing?" she asked.

"That's the third thing. If I don't want to destroy my clothes, I have to get naked before I shift. Turn around if you want."

He was pleased when she didn't turn around. He unfastened his pants and shoved them down. No need to take off underwear; he usually went commando.

When he was fully nude, he said, "Ready?"

She nodded, her eyes locked on his face. He tried not to grin, because he could tell she wanted to look at all of him, but she was resisting so hard.

Closing his eyes, he dropped to all fours and called his wolf forward. The brilliant light of the shift was visible through his eyelids. He felt his spine bow and shift, followed by his shoulders. The rest of his bones snapped and reformed, and his muscles lengthened and rearranged themselves. His skin itched as fur sprouted.

Before the shift was over, he opened his eyes, hoping to catch a glimpse of Jessica through the white energy that surrounded him. All he could make out was her silhouette, but she hadn't moved. He hadn't scared her off, yet. Maybe it would be better for her if he did scare her off. If she ran away now, she wouldn't have time to get attached to him.

The light faded and he had an unobstructed view of her. He rolled his neck, stretched forward to work the kinks out of his back—it had been awhile since he'd taken his wolf form.

"Wow," Jessica breathed.

He sensed no fear in her, and even though he'd been half-hoping for her to run a moment ago, he was glad she wasn't afraid. He closed the distance between them with a few steps, then stood in front of her, waiting to see what she'd do.

"You're so pretty," she said.

He snorted, and she laughed.

"Can I pet you?"

He always wanted her to touch him. Always. He bumped his muzzle against her hand and she reached her fingers out to stroke his fur.

"Incredible," she murmured.

In his wolf form, he could better see, hear, and smell. Her heartbeat was faster than normal, but not alarmingly so. She wasn't scared; she was excited.

"I wish I could turn into a wolf," she said.

He wished she could, too, but shifters were born, not bitten like in the movies. But it didn't matter to him if she was a shifter or not—she was a part of his pack forever, even if she never knew it.

He walked in a circle around her, proud of how steady his gait was, even with his forepaw gone. As he moved, she ran her fingers through his coat.

"What's that?" she asked.

He looked up to see what she was talking about. The notebook and books were still on the rock where he'd left them. She walked over to them and picked them up.

"*The Botany of Desire*," she murmured. "This has been on my to-read list for ages. And *Leaves of Grass*, I don't know about that one. I don't get poetry. But this guidebook, whoa!"

She looked at Marcus and he stared back.

"Did you get these for me?" she asked.

When he nodded, she fell to her knees and wrapped her

arms around him. The only person to hug him in his wolf form had been Marianne when she was small, and he would've thought a hug from an adult would be weird, even unwelcome. But instead, he reveled in Jessica's embrace.

"Thank you," she whispered.

He nudged the notebook with his snout, so she set down the other books and picked it up.

Her eyes widened as she flipped through the pages. "Wow, Marcus. This is amazing."

He'd affixed several different leaves from plants in the area to each page, and she ran her fingers over their shapes.

"I love it," she said.

Marcus closed his eyes and shifted back into his human form. The pain of shifting barely registered because he had his intentions on one thing only—holding Jessica.

Her eyes were large with appreciation as she took in his naked form. This time she didn't focus only on his face; she let her gaze travel over his entire body.

"This is incredible," she said. "*You're* incredible. Not just the wolf. But the way you thought of me. You considered what I like. This is the best gift I've ever been given."

"You should get to learn about things that make you happy," he said, feeling uncomfortable. He didn't mind her physical scrutiny, but her little peeks into his heart were opening him up, and they left him feeling exposed.

She took a step closer to him, and then another. Her gaze was soft, her lips still swollen from the bruising kiss he'd given her not half an hour ago.

"Jessica," he said, his voice rough.

"Yes," she said. "The answer's yes. Whatever you're about to ask me, the answer is yes."

He reached for her and she went into his arms, standing on her tiptoes and tilting her face toward his. He grabbed the back of her neck, gripping her so he could move her mouth just the way he needed it—the angle perfect for fitting his lips over hers and kissing her deeply, drinking her in, showing her just how much he wanted her.

Her syrupy sweet taste was like a drug. Need built in him, but he had to keep her safe, too.

"Get in the trailer," he said as he pulled away from her decadent mouth. "Wait for me. I have to get something and I'll be back in five minutes."

She nodded as if in a daze, her cheeks flushed, her eyes half-closed. She turned around to go to the trailer, and then turned to look over her shoulder at him.

"Am I imagining this?" she asked.

He shook his head. "It's real. I'll be back in a few."

Falling to his knees in the pine needles, he let his wolf return. It wasn't easy to shift again so soon after transforming, but his wolf was faster, and he didn't want to keep his woman waiting.

15

J essica stepped into the trailer, seeing it in a new light. This was finally happening. And it was happening in this cozy, sweet little camp trailer where they'd first met. Well, where they'd first truly met, when she wasn't drunk and half out of her mind with terror.

He'd slept with her that night, his body next to hers. She hadn't thought about that before, how they'd woken up together. How protected she'd felt.

And the way he had kissed her just now. She'd felt elevated. Cherished.

This man was going to ruin her for all other men...and she would enjoy every second of it.

His shadow passed over the trailer's curtained window, and then he said, "It's me," outside the door before pushing it open.

He stood before her, naked as before, and holding a box of condoms.

"Shifters can't get or transmit STDs," he said, "but I can get you pregnant. And either way, I want you to feel safe."

She nodded. "Thank you."

Taking three steps, he was right in front of her again, just inches away. "Do you want this, Jessica?"

His body heat reached through her clothes, warming her skin. Barely able to speak, she whispered, "Yes."

"I think you should take this off, then." He fingered the sleeve of her top, his touch so light it caused goosebumps to form on her arms.

Nodding, Jessica reached for the hem.

"Let me?" he asked.

She nodded again.

He undressed her slowly, kissing every bit of skin he exposed as he reverently removed her shirt, then her shorts. He knelt on the ground in front of her, cupped her ass with his hand, and pressed his head to her lower stomach. There, he closed his eyes and breathed in deeply.

"You smell so fucking good," he said, rubbing his face against her belly. His whiskers were pleasantly scratchy.

She twined her fingers in his brown locks, feeling their softness against her skin.

"Back you go," he said, pushing her carefully toward the bed.

She moved until the backs of her knees hit the cushion, then she sat down.

"Off with these." He tugged at the edge of her panties.

She lifted her hips to allow them off.

He breathed in again, his gaze warm and dark against her mound. "I'm going to feast on you."

"O-okay," she said.

"Your job," he said, trailing his hand up her leg, slowly, so slowly, "is to tell me what you like and what you don't like."

His gray eyes stared directly into hers.

"Got it," she said, barely able to speak. Arcs of pleasure shot through her, just from the barest touch of his hand on her leg, moving ever closer, ever more firmly toward her pussy.

He breathed out against her and she shivered again. She tried not to move too much, but she wanted his mouth on her.

"No more teasing," she begged.

He smiled and rubbed his face against her inner thigh. "All right, Jessica."

While she liked their inside joke with the wrong names, she loved that right now, she was *Jessica*. She was really herself, and this was really happening.

And then his mouth was *there*, right where she needed it, his lips and tongue slippery and warm and wet against her center, loving her, tugging moans from her lips, driving her wild.

"Please," she whispered. "Please, please, please."

She didn't know what she was asking for, but she had a feeling he was the only man in the world who could give it to her.

"I got you," he whispered against her skin. "You can come, Jessica."

She was so close to that precipice, almost there, wound so tightly her muscles strained and she wondered how she didn't crush his head between her thighs, she was holding so tightly to him.

He pressed a finger inside of her and licked her again, sucking gently on her clit while he slid his finger against her walls. She gripped the blankets and gasped, the sensations so strong, so wonderful.

"Yes," she said, "there, please, yes—"

The release was pure ecstasy, her body bursting in pleasure and relief. She shook and cried out. Then she leaned up on her elbows and tried to catch her breath.

Keeping his finger inside of her, Marcus looked up, his gray eyes intent on hers.

"More?" he asked.

"Yes." She gripped his biceps and tugged.

Although she'd never be strong enough to budge this giant of a man, he read her intention and slid his body over hers until he hovered over her. His cock was hard against her lower stomach. She reached down to slide her hand over the silky length.

When he groaned, her lower stomach tightened in anticipation.

"Just a second," he said, reaching back for the condoms and pulling one from the box.

She watched, her body alight, while he unwrapped the condom and rolled it over his cock. His eyes never left hers as he gave himself a squeeze. That big, rough hand, that big cock. Jessica couldn't wait for it any longer. She grabbed his hips and yanked him forward, felt his tip at her entrance.

"Are you ready?" he asked, his voice gruff.

"Yes." She tugged him forward again.

He slid into her slowly. He was thicker than she'd expected, filling her to the point of discomfort, but he moved with control and she stretched around his girth.

"Doing okay?" he asked.

She grinned up at him, then leaned forward to kiss his mouth.

"Better than okay," she said, falling back again.

He skimmed his hand over her breasts, lingering on one nipple, then the other. Then he began a slow drag in and out of her, his cock pressing forward, then pulling back out again. Locking her legs around his waist, she met his thrusts.

"I'm going to—again," she said.

"You never told me what you liked, when I was licking your pussy," he said, leaning down to gently bite her neck.

"I liked it all," she said.

"Did you like it when I sucked your clit?"

The very reminder set her clit to throbbing all over again. "Yes," she gasped.

Pulling up from her slightly, he said, "Will you play with your clit now, so I can watch?"

She nodded, but she felt shy as she reached down to touch herself.

"So beautiful." His voice was full of admiration. He kept up his relentless, slow stroking.

She was going to come again. Rubbing herself, combined with the fullness he gave her, was getting her there. She continued lifting her hips in time to his movements.

When she closed her eyes, he said, "Look at me, Jessica. I want to see your eyes this time, when you come on my cock."

She opened her eyes, and that was it. His gray gaze filled her vision as she flew into the heights of ecstasy, her whole body rippling and throbbing with the release. He tensed up against her for his last thrusts, and she felt his cock pulsing within as he came, too.

He fell carefully against her, embracing her, his chest pressed to hers.

"Jessica," he said softly, her name muffled as he spoke into her neck.

Little shivers worked through her body as she came

down from her orgasm, but Marcus's arms held her tightly. He rolled over to his side, tucking her against him.

"Gotta deal with the condom," he muttered, slowly getting up.

He was back a second later, right where he'd left off, and he tugged her against him. She fell into a blissful sleep with his breath gently moving against her hair.

16

When Marcus woke up, he inhaled deeply. Flowery notes of freesia filled his nose. Jessica was snuggled against him, her long lashes gracing her cheeks while she slept. She was so beautiful, and she'd come apart so perfectly in his arms last night.

He sensed the moment that she woke. Her breathing changed slightly, and she stretched with her eyes closed. Her hand searched him out, and she draped herself over his chest, throwing her leg over his waist for good measure. When he pressed the hardness of his dick against her thigh, her eyes opened.

"Well, hello there," she said in a sleepy voice. She was naked, and so was he. Neither of them had dressed after sex last night—which was just how he liked it.

"Good morning, Juanita."

She grinned. "Good morning, Midas."

She didn't say anything about his boner, but she pushed her leg down a little harder. Marcus groaned.

"You're giving me some very good ideas," he said.

"Really?"

"Yeah." He ran his hand over the curve of her hip.

"Then I'm doing something right."

He chuckled. "What's your favorite position?"

Her gaze got even more mischievous. "How about I show you?"

Fuck yes, that sounded good to him.

She sat up and climbed on top of his lap, rubbing her naked pussy over his dick. He slid through her folds easily— she was already wet. His cock pulsed, eager.

"Condom," he growled.

She reached back for the box and got one. After unwrapping it, she rolled it onto his cock. Her touch was heaven. She sat up on her knees, then held his dick in her hand to guide it inside of her.

He feasted his gaze on her curvy body, loving the way her breasts hung, full and tipped with rosy brown nipples, loving the way her stomach moved as she fit over him, her pussy squeezing his dick as she adjusted.

Reaching between her legs, he thumbed her clit. She gasped and braced herself with her hands on his shoulders, then began to move over him in earnest, her hips rolling.

Her breasts were right in front of his face. He sat up enough that he could pull one of her nipples into his mouth. When he sucked hard, she moved faster.

"Yes," she said. "Yes, please, more of that, oh my—"

He sucked hard again, and she cried out. Her pussy milked him, rippling squeezes that stole his orgasm in a torrent of pleasure.

She fell against his chest. He remained inside of her, feeling her twitch around him as they each caught their breath.

"I like doing it your way," he murmured.

"Good." She kissed his shoulder, then gingerly crawled

off of him. A satisfied smile on her lips, she stretched and swung her legs over the side of the trailer bed. "I guess we should get to training?"

"I don't know about you, but I like the practice we're doing right here." He captured her in his arms and tugged her back to kiss her neck.

"How long until they fight for Blythe?" she asked.

"We have a little more than a week."

"Then we should train." Her voice was filled with regret.

Marcus felt the same—it was more important to get in shape to save her friend. Still, he didn't know how many days like this he would get with Jessica. He couldn't find it in him to regret anything they had done last night, or this morning, but the fact remained that she belonged outside of this territory and he belonged within it.

They had no future, and that gutted him.

After a breakfast of fruit and English muffins, they went outside. The morning air was cool, but it didn't seem too chilly for Jessica, and he was glad for that. He still felt bad every time he thought about throwing her in the lake. Thankfully, if last night had been any indication, she didn't hold a grudge.

The front door of Caitlyn and Grant's cabin opened and Grant walked outside. He waved before continuing to his garage.

Jessica turned and faced Marcus. She planted her feet hip width apart and kept her arms loose at her sides, just like he had taught her. A challenging smile spread across her face and she raised an eyebrow. "Are you ready, old man?"

"Always." He winked at her.

She launched herself at him and he blocked her attack.

Spinning, he got behind her and hugged her against his front.

"Dang it," she panted. "I do that every single time."

He pressed himself against her ass. "I appreciate your predictability."

She leaned against him, soft curves to his hard front. He nipped her ear, enjoying her soft gasp.

"Who's your friend, Marcus?"

The voice came from behind. Marcus spun around, keeping Jessica on the other side of him, away from danger. Jase walked forward through the trees, his sandalwood scent coming with him. His dark eyebrows were high on his forehead, showcasing his surprise.

Several curses were on the tip of Marcus's tongue, but he couldn't bring himself to speak. His mind worked frantically as he tried to come up with the best excuse for Jessica being here. He briefly entertained the notion of trying to convince Jase that she wasn't here at all. But he knew that wouldn't work.

Her presence here was no longer a secret.

She was in more danger than ever. He hadn't been careful enough, he'd failed her.

Jessica tried to come around Marcus. He tried to block her, but she shoved his arm down. It was too late, anyway. The damage was done.

She faced Jase, her stubborn chin jutting out. "I'm Jessica Valdez. Who are you?"

"Jase Englender." He took a step toward them. He had one gold eye, one green, and both were staring hard at Jessica.

Marcus growled, low in his throat.

"He's one of the good guys, right?" Jessica asked.

"I don't think any of us can be considered good—"

Marcus began.

But Jessica was already striding forward, her right hand outstretched.

Chuckling, Jase shook her hand. He said, "You guys want to tell me what's going on?"

"Not really." Marcus frowned.

"Looks to me like someone else came into our territory the night Blythe arrived," Jase said. "Looks to me, Marcus, like you tried to keep her a secret."

"Is it any fuckin' surprise?" Marcus asked. "Look what's happening to her friend right now."

Jase held up his hands. "I don't blame you. I think this was smart. Problem is, it's no long-term solution."

"We're aware of that," Jessica said.

"So," Jase said, "what's the plan?"

Jessica spoke before Marcus could. "We're asking a witch to intervene. When she sees that Blythe and I are here by mistake, we think she'll let us out."

Jase nodded, but he was frowning. "Witches aren't known for doing favors."

"Well, it's the only idea we have," Marcus said, "unless you have a suggestion?"

"Unfortunately, no, I don't." Jase took in a big breath and let it out slowly. He gave Jessica an evaluating look, a look Marcus wasn't so sure he liked. Then he said in a serious voice, "Is Marcus treating you okay?"

Marcus's respect for Jase increased. Jase was taking care of Blythe, and he was showing concern for Jessica. He knew Jase had designs on making the Junkyard a better place, gathering some of the shifters together. It seemed to Marcus that Jase was a natural leader, and he had a good heart.

"Yeah, he's treating me well," Jessica said.

"Glad to hear it," Jase said. "You need anything?"

"A practice partner, to fight with Marcus," she said. "He's going to try to win Blythe for me, but I'm no good at helping him practice."

A smile spread across Jase's face. "I'll be fighting for her too."

"What?" Jessica said, all goodwill gone as she jabbed a finger in Jase's chest. "You keep your hands off of her."

Jase laughed, his teeth white against his tanned skin. "Easy, there. I'm fighting for the same reason you are. To keep her away from those other assholes."

Jessica's shoulders relaxed, and she backed up until she stood against Marcus. "Okay, then. But if you hurt her..."

THE NEXT FEW hours passed quickly, with Marcus and Jase sparring. Jessica watched for the most part, adding commentary from time to time, and cheering for Marcus.

"You were holding back on me," she said at one point.

Marcus shrugged. He wasn't going to lie to her. But there was no way he would come after Jessica with the same force he would use on Jase. As far as Jase's abilities, he was a damn good fighter. Maybe not as good as Carter, but Carter was an anomaly. Until Lena, Carter had spent every waking moment fighting.

Sweaty and exhausted, Jase finally said goodbye, leaving Marcus and Jessica alone.

Jessica marched over to Marcus, arms outstretched for a hug. Then she stopped suddenly, wrinkling her nose. "Ew. You're all sweaty. It looks sexy, but I don't want to hug you."

Marcus pretended to reach for her, and she squealed.

"Maybe we can sneak down to the lake," he said. "We can both cool off."

"Do you think it's safe?" Jessica asked.

"I can scout ahead. The shore curves at one point, protecting it from view. Lots of trees in the way. What do you think?"

She agreed, so Marcus hurried off to make sure the coast was clear. He checked, and double checked. No one was nearby.

He returned with Jessica, bringing her to a part of the shore that was guarded by a thick grove of trees. Not wasting any time, he took off his shirt and pants and jumped in the water. It was cool, but not cold, a balm to his overheated muscles. When he came to the surface, he was pleased to see Jessica standing on a flat rock wearing only her bra and underwear.

"What do you say, Jill?" he called. "Are you coming in?"

In answer, she jumped from the rock, landing close to him, her splash catching him in the face. Her head broke the surface a moment later. She was grinning.

"This is way better than last time," she said.

"I still feel bad about that." Marcus couldn't resist. He reached out and tugged her into his arms.

She splayed her hands over his chest, sliding them over his skin. Her gaze was lowered like she was thinking about something.

"What is it?" he asked.

"I'm thinking about Jase. Are you sure he's not going to hurt Blythe, if he wins?"

Marcus nodded and took one of her hands in his. "I'm sure of it. I can tell when someone's lying, remember?"

She looked up at him then, her brown eyes searching. "Can you really?" she asked in a skeptical voice. "Have you tested this?"

"No need to test it," he said. "It just is."

"I won an essay contest when I was eight."

She was testing him. He didn't mind playing along. "That's the truth."

"It was an argumentative essay that my parents made me write to convince them to extend my bedtime." She spoke with a straight face and without a hitch in her voice, but he could sense a difference.

"There's a lie in there somewhere," he said.

Grinning, she said, "I'm impressed. It was an argumentative essay, but I was campaigning for sugary cereal."

He laughed. "You're still lying to me."

"Damn, you're good. I was trying to get my babysitter fired."

"The babysitter was that bad, huh?" Marcus asked.

"The worst. She actually made me do my homework."

"Intolerable," Marcus said.

Jessica laughed. "She was. But only because it was really my parents who I wanted around."

"That makes sense. So you and your parents weren't close?"

"Eh." She dove under the water and swam a small lap around Marcus. When she came up again, she wiped the water droplets from her face and said, "We weren't close in the ways that counted. They love me, and I love them, but they don't get me."

"What do you mean?" Marcus asked. He didn't like the defeated expression on her face.

She shrugged. "It's kind of dumb. I mean, they took care of me. They were champs in that regard. I had a nice house, food to eat, and all the support I needed in school. So really, I don't feel like I have room to complain. Not when so many people have less."

"The thing about pain," Marcus said in a quiet voice, "is

that it fills whatever space it has. Whether or not other people are worse off, it still hurts you."

She nodded thoughtfully. "So you're saying that even though others are struggling with more, it's okay for me to recognize the pain of what I'm feeling."

"Yeah. There's probably always going to be someone who's worse off. But it doesn't minimize what you're going through."

"I just don't want to be a spoiled little rich girl." She wrinkled her nose, like the phrase was distasteful.

"Someone has called you that before," he guessed.

She flipped around and floated on her back. Staring at the sky, she said, "My dad did, yeah. He was mad when I didn't want to go to this writing camp."

"But if writing isn't your thing..."

"Exactly. They're authors, and that's great for them. And with their contacts in New York publishing, not to mention the hype that could be built up just because I have their name, I could write and publish books, too."

He was starting to wonder just who her parents were. "Wait a second. You said your last name is Valdez. Are your parents—"

"Carlos and Donna," she said. "Yeah."

He wasn't a big reader, but he'd heard of them. Their books were frequently turned into movies or streaming series on Netflix.

"I bet having famous parents makes for a lonely childhood," he said.

"It doesn't have to, but it did for me," she said. "Anyway, that's why the books and the notebook you gave me are so perfect. I feel like for the first time someone that I care about actually knows me. Or is at least trying to, you know?"

"Yeah. I know."

They spent the next hour swimming and floating on their backs in the lake, until Jessica got too cold, and it was time to go back to the trailer. The whole time though, Marcus was conscious of the fact that she didn't have anybody else who could love her as much as he was starting to.

17

Two days later, Jessica awoke with Marcus's arms wrapped tightly around her. She kissed his forearm.

She knew the big fight was coming up. She knew they had to rescue Blythe. She knew there were dozens of reasons that she shouldn't be falling in love with this man.

And yet...she was falling in love with this man.

She had been in love before, or she had thought it was love before—brief infatuations with boys in school, far away crushes on guys at college. She knew she had a tendency to latch on too quickly. Even as she enjoyed Marcus's embrace, she tried to remind herself of that fact.

The birds outside the trailer sang their morning chorus. Marcus's hand was curled around her hip, warm and possessive. He had given her so much over the past few days. He'd given her his time, his attention, his affection. She suspected that despite the short time they had been together, he knew her better than anyone else knew her.

Yet she sensed, despite everything he was giving her, he was holding a part of himself back.

Jessica would have to try to hold herself back, too.

She carefully climbed out of bed. She found a pair of pants and a shirt and put them on.

Marcus stretched and watched her get dressed. "Do you have to put clothes on?" he asked.

"Yes, we need to train. Do you think Jase will join us again?"

Jase had come yesterday, and he and Marcus had trained for hours. Jessica was impressed. Jase didn't even know Blythe, yet he seemed one hundred percent invested in protecting and defending her.

"I'm not sure," Marcus said.

Jessica turned toward the kitchen counter to fix them some breakfast, but Marcus grabbed her hip and swung her back toward him.

His gray eyes were soft with tenderness—a tenderness that felt sharp against her heart.

"Are you doing okay?" he asked.

"Yeah, I'm great." She tried to move away. There was breakfast to make, and her heart to protect.

"We established I can tell when you're lying."

Well, that was hardly fair. She couldn't bear to tell him the truth—that she was falling for him. She was already weaker than him, being smaller, being human. Why should he also get the advantage in their relationship, or whatever this was?

"Julie." His voice was firm. "You're thinking a lot. Do you want to share with the rest of the class?"

She stared at him. "Not really."

He let go of her with a sigh. "Fair enough."

She moved away then, over to the kitchen. Coffee would help, even if it tasted like mud.

As she worked, she was very aware of Marcus watching

her from the bed. His chest was bare, and he leaned up on one arm. His gray gaze was soft, contemplative. Dark scruff decorated his cheeks. She wondered when he shaved. He had to, occasionally, or he would already have a full beard by now. Clean-shaven or stubbly, he was the handsomest man she had ever seen or ever would see. Her heart squeezed painfully in her chest.

Why did love have to hurt so much?

THANKFULLY, sparring took most of Jessica's attention over the course of the morning. There simply wasn't time to mope about unrequited love when she was dodging Marcus's hits. She wished she was stronger so that he could use more of his skill and strength with her during training. Sadly, though, he would have to make do with her until someone better came along.

The thought made her freeze. Was that why he held himself back from her? Was he waiting for someone better to come along? Not to spar with, but to love and care for?

The idea made her gut churn, so she shoved it to the back of her mind.

"Time for a break," Marcus said.

Jessica didn't want a break. Fighting was the only thing that kept her from thinking.

Ignoring his request, she threw a punch at him and made contact with his chest. She suspected it hurt her hand more than it hurt him.

"You're feisty this morning," he said.

"Maybe. Or maybe I have more energy than you, old man."

"Aw, Joan, you're in trouble now."

He picked her up, and she squealed. They were both sweaty, and a part of her was grossed out by that, but mostly she didn't mind. Holding her tight, he walked them over to the old picnic chair leaning against the trailer.

"Will that hold us?" she asked as he eased down, cradling her to his chest.

"Sure, it'll hold us."

No sooner had he settled his weight all the way into it, than the porch chair collapsed. They fell into a heap, and once Jessica realized she hadn't been hurt, and Marcus hadn't been either, she started laughing. He laughed too, his smile so carefree that it caused her breath to hitch with a pleasure-pain so acute, her laughing immediately stopped.

This was not going to end well.

Instead of getting up, he kept her cradled against him. She was quickly becoming addicted to this feeling of being embraced by Marcus.

"Are you going to tell me what's bothering you yet?" he asked.

Not this again. She didn't want to talk about it—the feelings were too raw. But there was something she could give him instead.

"I don't know that much about you," she said. "You hold yourself back. I've told you all about my childhood, but I don't know very much about your past."

She felt the movement of his chest as he nodded.

"I told you how I came to be here," he said.

"Tell me more about your sister."

Some of the tension melted out of him. In a softer voice, he said, "She's amazing. I'd do anything for her."

"Does she turn into a wolf like you?" Jessica asked.

"No, she's human. Like you. She's my half-sister, and

quite a bit younger than me. We have the same mom, different dads."

Jessica leaned her head back against his shoulder. "Is your dad still around?"

"Not so much, no. He didn't really love my mom—she wasn't his mate. What they had was a fling, I guess, and I wasn't really planned. He stuck around long enough to set me up with a local pack, so they could help me learn how to be a wolf shifter. Last time I saw him, I was fifteen or so."

As far as Jessica was concerned, the man had to be an idiot if he didn't want to hang around his son. Marcus was one of the best people she knew. But Marcus didn't seem that upset by it, so she waited to see if he'd say anything else.

"Anyway, my mom met my stepdad, fell in love, got married. They had Marianne. Before I had a sister, it bothered me that my dad didn't want to stick around. But as soon as Marianne showed up, I felt like I had all I needed."

"She must be really special," Jessica said.

"She is. She makes me laugh, kind of like you do. She likes to test my shifter abilities, just like you did at the lake the other day."

Jessica laughed, then she said, "You said something weird a minute ago. You said your mom wasn't your dad's mate?"

"Yeah. It's a shifter thing."

She waited for him to elaborate, but he didn't. Instead, he helped Jessica off his lap and stood. "I should make us some lunch."

"Want some help?" she asked.

"No, you fixed breakfast. I'll take care of lunch."

There was tenderness in his eyes as he spoke, and some sorrow, too. Jessica wondered what caused it. He must have been missing his sister. And maybe there was more to missing his dad than he had said.

She leaned against the side of the trailer. Her new nature notebook was inside. Maybe she should get it, make some notes on the leaves Marcus had gathered. Then again, it was really nice sitting out here in the sun. It felt warm against her face, like Marcus's touch. She closed her eyes and decided to enjoy it.

"I thought you said there weren't any women in there."

The unfamiliar feminine voice made Jessica jump up and she looked wildly around. Two women stood on the other side of the gravel line. One had blue eyes and shoulder-length brown hair pulled back in a ponytail. The other had blond hair and stood a good six inches taller than Jessica and the brunette.

Remembering how nice Caitlyn had been, Jessica hurried over to them.

"Hey," she said. "I'm Jessica."

The brown-haired woman spoke. "I'm Lena. This is Allison. Um, we're looking for Marcus?"

Jessica cocked her head, reevaluating the women. What did they want with Marcus?

The blonde, Allison, turned to Lena. "There's a male wolf's scent all over her. Is that Marcus's scent?"

Jessica wasn't sure what to say. She didn't know how someone would smell Marcus on her unless they were shifter. The flash of competitive jealousy in Allison's eyes made Jessica glad she wore Marcus's scent.

Lena chewed her lip thoughtfully, but her eyes were friendly as they evaluated Jessica. "Yes, it is his scent."

Jessica looked from one woman to the other, then said, "I'll, uh...I'll go get him."

Before Jessica could turn around, Lena looked past Jessica and her expression brightened.

"Hey, Marcus," Lena said with a little wave.

Marcus was hurrying toward them. He stopped next to Jessica. She wondered why he didn't hold her hand. If they had been alone, he would have touched her. He was always touching her. So why not now?

She shook it off. She was overanalyzing this.

"Hi, Lena," Marcus said.

"Hey," Lena said slowly. "I was just stopping by for a visit, with my new friend Allison."

Could Jessica feel Marcus tensing up beside her? Or was that just her imagination? She willed her brain to stop thinking and analyzing everything.

"Hey," Marcus said to Allison.

Jessica did not miss the way Allison's eyes appraised Marcus. And she didn't at all like the way Allison frowned when she focused on his right wrist, where his hand used to be.

Still, Allison's voice was flirtatious as she responded, "Hi. We were just meeting your...friend. Jennifer, is that right?"

Finally, finally Marcus put his arm around Jessica's shoulders and drew her closer to his side.

"Jessica," he said, at the same time Jessica corrected her.

Jessica peeked up at him. His face was impassive, showing no emotion whatsoever.

Lena spoke next. "Do the others know about her?"

"Only Jase," Jessica said. "I've been hiding in the trailer, and we're hoping nobody comes around."

"Lena, well, it's good to see you," Marcus said, "but Jessica and I are just about to have lunch."

"Sure," Lena said. "Do you mind if I have a quick word, though?"

Jessica knew when she was being dismissed, but she didn't budge until Allison walked away, too.

Jessica had nearly reached the trailer when she heard Marcus say, "I told you I don't need your matchmaking, Lena."

"Well, how was I to know you had a woman squirreled away in the trailer?" she asked.

Matchmaking? Jessica liked this less and less. Maybe Marcus didn't want Jessica around long-term, but right now, he was hers.

18

Marcus's wolf growled at the unhappy expression Jessica wore as she walked off toward the trailer. Allison didn't look any happier to be dismissed, either, but that didn't bother him in the slightest.

"I don't have a woman squirreled away in the trailer," he told Lena.

She folded her arms over her chest and gave a pointed look to where Jessica was opening the trailer door and stepping inside.

Marcus ran a hand over his whiskers. "She wasn't here before," he said. "Besides, whether or not she's here, I don't want you bringing women here to meet me. I don't need a mate, and I'm not getting out."

"I can't accept that." Lena's blue eyes flashed. "You don't belong here. I know it, Carter knows it, and Grant and Caitlyn know it, too."

A week ago, Marcus would have argued with her. But now he was just tired. And even worse, the traitorous part of his heart was grasping at the hope that maybe she was right.

Maybe he didn't belong in here. Maybe he could get out—with Jessica. Just because the boundary hadn't let him through before, didn't mean the witch wouldn't.

Lena went on, "Anyway, I won't bring anybody else."

Marcus stared at her. What wasn't she saying? It was unlike her to give up so easily.

"I appreciate that," he said. "But...why?"

She smirked. "Seems like you didn't need my help, after all."

With that, she spun on her heel and joined Allison at the far edge of the clearing. Allison gestured toward Marcus, obviously annoyed, but Lena just smiled and shrugged, then the two of them walked away.

Sighing, Marcus returned to the trailer. Jessica stepped lightly out of it, bearing their two plates with sandwiches, and a deep scowl.

"So, Maurice, do you want to tell me what that was all about?" she asked.

"Nothing important," he said.

She pushed out her chin, and he knew she was going to start being stubborn. "Why don't you enlighten me, and let me decide whether or not it's important?"

She was so fucking sexy when she was pissy.

He cocked his head at her. "You jealous, Joanne?"

"You wish," she said shortly.

He couldn't help smiling. When had anyone been jealous over him? Just about never. He couldn't deny this was helping his ego. Still, she was obviously upset, so he couldn't enjoy it as much as he wanted to.

"Come here, Jessica." He took the plates from her one at a time, then set them on a fallen log. She turned around, trying to ignore him, but he put his hand on her shoulder and gave her a gentle massage. She was tense. Pissed.

She really was jealous, he realized. Painfully so. His amusement faded and he tugged her over, pulling her into a hug.

"I'm sorry for making fun of you," he said. "I didn't mean to upset you."

"You didn't upset me," she said. "They did. I don't even know why they were here."

He sighed. "Lena's a friend of mine. She's trying to find me a mate."

"Do you want a mate?"

"No, I didn't. I told her to stop bringing women around."

He could sense that she had more questions, so he waited. But if she had more questions, she kept them locked up in that pretty mouth.

He knew it was risky, and he didn't want to give her any false hope of forever, but he couldn't resist squeezing her tight and murmuring, "The only one I want is you."

NOTHING OVERTLY CHANGED BETWEEN THEM, no declarations had been made. But at the end of the day, Marcus couldn't keep from touching her at every opportunity. Her curvy body, her quiet smiles, her teasing laughter, her unadulterated joy in the natural world, her heated expression as their gazes met—each of those things alone could make him pause and take note. But put together into the singular package that was Jessica? They'd bring him to his fucking knees.

The door had barely closed after they went into the trailer before Marcus tugged on the edge of Jessica's shirt. "I need you," he said, his voice hoarse with want.

Her eyes grew round and her sweet scent strengthened

in his nose. Gaze never leaving his, she pulled her shirt over her head.

"You need me?"

"Yes." He grabbed her waist, held her neck in his hand and kissed her plump lips, thrusting his tongue between them.

She moaned and pulled back. "I'm yours, Marcus."

His need for her transcended sex. He didn't just want to chase fleeting pleasure. He needed a forever.

He needed what he could not have.

Gripping his face in her hands, she brought his mouth to hers again. As he kissed her, he unsnapped her bra and pulled the straps down her shoulders to free her from it. Next, he shoved down her shorts, the panties with them. She kicked them away, along with her shoes and socks.

Now she was naked in his arms. His inner wolf howled. She belonged here with him, like this. He'd keep her for as long as possible.

She was shoving down his pants, yanking on his shirt, unable to get his clothes off. He briefly let her go to help out with the onerous task of undressing. Her hands were smooth against his chest and arms as she explored his body. She ran a hand down over his abs to where his cock jutted eagerly forward.

"Do you want to use this on me?" she whispered.

"Fuck yes," he said, thrusting into her grip.

When she reached down and scratched her fingernails lightly against his balls, he groaned with pleasure and crowded her against the wall, licking and sucking her neck. The box of condoms rested on the counter next to him so he pulled one out, unwrapped it, and rolled it over his cock. Jessica watched, her lips slightly parted, a flush of pink darkening her tanned skin.

Once he'd made himself safe for her, he nudged her legs apart and picked her up, using the wall and one of his legs to hold her at the perfect height so he could slide into her wet heat.

"Marcus," she gasped.

He pumped inside her, but heard a loud knocking sound —her head was hitting the wall.

"Sorry," he said, and carried her to the bed.

"I didn't mind." Her voice was breathless.

"I never want to hurt you," he said, his heart swelling as he spoke the words. "Ever."

He stroked his hand and arm over her skin, kissed her mouth, treasured every gasp and sigh she made. He caressed her breasts, tugged lightly on her nipples, felt her tighten around him.

His mouth against her neck and shoulder gave him an unnameable need. He wanted to mark her, bite her hard enough to scar so he and everyone else would know that they belonged to each other. The temptation was too great, with her sweet-smelling skin so close to his mouth. He pulled back so he was kneeling, then lifted each of her legs and hooked them over his shoulders.

"Oh—fuck—wow," Jessica said. "That angle."

He kept his strokes even and purposeful, not ready to lose control yet. Her pussy tightened around him and she grabbed his forearms, her nails scraping his skin.

"Marcus," she said. "I'm coming—"

"Yes. Come on my dick, squeeze me tight." He held one of her legs on his shoulder with his arm, and with his hand, he reached down to rub his thumb over her clit.

She wailed as she came, her hands digging into his hips while he continued to thrust. As her pussy squeezed him rhythmically, he came, too, the orgasm stretching through his whole body until it burst forth.

After he got up and disposed of the condom, he returned to the cramped little bed and pulled Jessica against him.

"Was that too much?" he asked.

"No," she said, pressing a kiss to his neck. "More. With you, I always want more."

Nothing had changed, yet things were very different. He felt closer to her, like he understood her better. He could sense her feelings, her wants, before she even gave voice to them. He had gone the last couple of months feeling like he had no purpose, but now he did. His purpose was Jessica.

When she got out of this place, he was going to be a wreck.

They spent the next day together, training and talking, scouring the area around the trailer for new plants, searching for them in the guidebook, and then recording them in Jessica's notebook. Marcus wasn't sure if he had ever even looked twice at a plant, but Jessica's enthusiasm was catching, and he found himself getting excited every time they thought they came upon something new.

Still, at this rate, they would be able to catalog every plant in the Junkyard in about a week. And then what? Jessica needed to be free of this place. She should be able to look for plants in other places, too.

He didn't want to, but he had to talk to Grant and find out if he'd heard from the witch yet. It was too late for Marcus—he was completely attached to Jessica. But if she could leave soon, maybe she wouldn't get too attached to him.

He kept an eye on Grant and Caitlyn's cabin, waiting for an opportunity to talk to Grant. However, it was Grant who came to him. He stood at the edge of the boundary, a strange expression on his face.

Marcus dropped the plant he had been holding and hurried over to talk to him, Jessica at his side.

"You have news," Marcus said.

"Yep."

Jessica was strangely quiet next to Marcus. He would have expected her to be jumping up and down, rocking on the balls of her feet, yelling at Grant to tell them the news already. Instead, she was quiet, thoughtful.

"The witch is dead." Grant rubbed a hand over the back of his neck. "No one else will talk to me. The entire coven is in mourning, apparently. A spokesperson said they aren't interested in shifter affairs."

"This isn't about shifters," Marcus said, unable to keep the anger from his voice. "This is about humans. Innocent humans."

"I get it, I really do," Grant said. "I just don't know what to tell you."

Jessica squeezed Marcus's forearm. "But Blythe..."

Marcus looked at her. "I know. And you, too."

"I don't care about me," she said, sounding just as angry as Marcus had a moment ago. "I'm not in danger. I'm fine. But if we don't win this fight, Blythe could get hurt."

"I won't let that happen," Marcus said.

Jessica pulled back, shaking her head. "This is too much."

"I know," he said. "I'm sorry."

"Not your fault. I just. Ugh." She covered her face with her hands. "It's hard to think any of this through. I need a minute."

She started walking away.

"Where are you going?" Marcus asked.

"I need to think," she said over her shoulder. "Just give me a minute to think."

Marcus turned back to Grant. "There's really nothing to do, is there?"

"You already tried to get out, alongside her?" Grant asked.

Marcus's heart squeezed painfully in his chest. "I did."

Grant looked from Marcus to Jessica's retreating figure. "Maybe it wouldn't hurt to try again. The way she looks at you, the way you look at her—"

Marcus shook his head. "Stop. I can't think about that. Besides, that won't help her friend."

Grant nodded. "True."

"Thanks for trying," Marcus said. It came out a growl, not because he was mad, but because he was upset.

As Grant walked away, Marcus realized he wasn't as upset as he probably should be. If Jessica couldn't get out, it meant she would still be here, with him. And a part of him was selfish enough to enjoy that idea.

Spinning around, he looked to see where Jessica had gone. She was nowhere in sight, but she couldn't have gotten far. She had said she wanted to think, but she was also hurting. He was torn between respecting her wishes and the need to comfort her. Deciding to give her a few more minutes, he headed toward the trailer. The sun was falling, the woods settling. He paused at the trailer door and cocked his head, listening. The woods were too quiet.

"Jessica?" he called softly.

Something was wrong. Very wrong. He tore off his shirt and yanked off his shoes and pants. Then he called forth his wolf.

The change was fast, spurred by panic. The white light

around him hadn't faded completely before he was lurching forward on partially shifted legs.

A sound reached him from the trees—a sound that just about ripped his soul in two.

Jessica, screaming.

19

Jessica's scream was real and raw. But as soon she let it out, she closed her mouth. Marcus would have heard that. Marcus would come for her. There was no doubt in her mind. Even if she wasn't his mate, even if he didn't want to be with her forever, he was a loyal, caring man. And he wouldn't leave her to fight off these two beasts on her own.

The leopard held back. It remained low to the ground, its focus on her, eyes unblinking. Its spotted coat was a thing of beauty, yet the danger it presented had her heart pounding with terror.

Unlike the leopard, the mountain lion moved, circling around to her right. Jessica guessed that the leopard was Fred Barnum. The mountain lion, she was less sure about. It could be the guy whose name started with a V. Vez-something. Most likely, though, it was Alleman; Marcus had warned her about him.

Whoever these guys were, they were not here to make friends.

Jessica had practiced fighting with Marcus—but only

while he was human. She had no idea how to fight off an animal. So far, neither one was attacking her. The mountain lion advanced, but it allowed her a step or two of her own for each one of his. She expected him to spring forward at any moment, but he didn't.

The leopard stood and moved with them. Then it sat, as if waiting for something.

What could it be waiting for? Marcus, maybe. But it seemed strange they weren't attacking. She would never be more defenseless than she was now. No weapon, no ally or hero. It was just her against two giant cats with sharp teeth and claws.

The mountain lion took another step. Jessica turned sideways, keeping him in her peripheral vision while she stepped away from him. He stepped forward again, and she repeated her action.

It wasn't until he moved forward once again that she realized what was happening.

They were herding her.

They'd already reached the outer edges of the dump, from what she could tell from the dark, hulking shapes at one side.

Her panic surged at the thought. She felt lightheaded, like she was watching this from somewhere else. These two big cats were stalking some other woman. Not Jessica. Jessica was safe at the trailer, Marcus at her side while they pored through the guidebook.

The leopard—or was it the mountain lion?—gave a soft growl.

Because the mountain lion looked away from Jessica, she guessed it was the leopard who had made the sound.

Both cats directed their attention to the woods.

Marcus was here.

It wasn't easy to see him in the darkness, but Jessica could still make out his eyes, glowing with fury. They burned with a righteous anger as he stalked toward the two big cats.

Without any warning, the leopard tore into the woods, straight at Marcus.

Jessica stifled a shriek of dismay. She couldn't bear to see Marcus get hurt, but what good could she be against vicious beasts?

The mountain lion, which had been closest to her, seemed content to watch the ensuing fight.

The leopard and the wolf hurtled toward each other, meeting in the air. Their movements were so swift, Jessica could barely track them. She held as still as possible, entranced by the display of violence and frozen by her fear of something happening to Marcus. She had never seen him look so strong, so enraged, so ferocious. He clamped his jaws onto the leopard's shoulder, then whipped his head to the side. The leopard flew a few feet before landing on its flank.

The leopard sprang up a second later, but the mountain lion was already on the move.

Jessica shouted a warning. Marcus was waiting, hackles raised, teeth bared.

With the two cats focused on Marcus, Jessica looked around frantically for a weapon. She would take anything, anything that could give her an advantage.

She ran to the nearest hulking structure in the dump. Closer up, she could see it was an old pick-up truck with a dangling front bumper. She reached down and tried to pry off the bumper, but it held fast on the other end. Tears of frustration filled her eyes, but she blinked them away. Looking to the side, she saw something slender jutting up from the mud. She grabbed it and it pulled free. It was a length of PVC pipe. Not as good as the metal pipe Blythe had in her RV, but it was all Jessica could find, and it would have to do. If she swung it with enough force, maybe it would do some damage.

Turning around, she raced toward the fight.

The leopard was down again, and it didn't look like he would be getting up, at least not anytime soon. Then again, Jessica had never seen one of these fights. She didn't really know.

Not willing to chance it, she stood behind the leopard. If he moved, she would whack him on the head.

The leopard's fur rose and fell with his breaths. Jessica divided her focus between the leopard and the fight between Marcus and the mountain lion.

The wolf and the mountain lion snarled and growled as they exchanged bites. The mountain lion raked his claws through Marcus's fur. Jessica saw blood. Terror thudded through her. He had to be okay. Maybe they should just run, retreat somewhere so they could be safe.

Instead of retreating, Marcus merely fought harder. He feinted one way, then leaped in the other direction. The mountain lion wasn't fast enough. Marcus caught him in the side, clamping his jaws down and not letting go.

The leopard at Jessica's feet stirred. Jessica took a deep breath. She had never hit anything in her life, except for Marcus while they were training, and the idea of doing it with the intent to harm now sickened her.

But when the leopard got to its feet and turned its great face to her, baring its fangs, she knew she had no choice. Using all her strength, she brought the pipe down on top of its head.

The pipe hit the leopard with a loud thud, and the leopard fell back down, its eyes rolling back before closing.

Breathing hard, Jessica looked back to where Marcus was fighting the mountain lion. At some point he had transferred his jaws to the mountain lion's throat. The mountain lion scrambled, kicking its legs but failing to get purchase. Marcus growled, and the mountain lion finally lay still beneath him.

As Jessica watched, a white light surrounded the mountain lion. Then, it was a man. He fit Marcus's description of Derrick Alleman—reddish blond hair, charcoal eyes.

The same strange white light surrounded Marcus as well. When it faded, Marcus stood. He kept his foot on Alleman's throat.

Both of them were bleeding, but not heavily. Marcus had a wound on his left shoulder that looked half-healed already.

"You can't have her," Marcus said. His voice sounded feral, low and wild.

"Looks like you won her, anyway," the other man said. "And we were going to sneak her in for us, not have to fight for her like Englender has us doing with the other one."

"Alleman, I mean it. You can't have her."

"Can I at least sit up?"

Marcus took his foot off of the man's neck, but he remained tense, his fist clenched.

The man shook his head and spit off to the side, then wiped some blood off his neck and chest. "That bitch told us it would be easy."

"Who?" Marcus asked.

Jessica's heart lurched. Surely Blythe hadn't given her away, had she? No. Unless they forced the information out of her, Blythe would never talk.

"A wolf bitch. She said she met you yesterday, and this one, too."

Allison. Jessica wished she could get out of the Junkyard for at least long enough to go kick that woman's ass. Marcus's scowl deepened, and she guessed he was feeling about the same.

He stepped back from Alleman. "Take Barnum and get the fuck out of my sight."

Jessica didn't expect Alleman to obey him, but he did. He walked over, naked as the day he was born, and picked up the unconscious leopard.

Jessica gripped her PVC pipe, ready to do whatever damage she was capable of. She would not be caught defenseless again. Not here, not anywhere.

Sneering at Jessica, he turned around and walked away.

Jessica looked at Marcus. He wasn't wearing any clothes, but that wasn't what she noticed the most. It was the look on his face, the mixture of fear and despair.

"They know you're here now." He closed his eyes.

"But you fought them off," she said, reliving the fear she'd experienced as he fought. "They left."

"They'll be back. The dominance I just fought for only lasts so long."

"How long does it last?" She took a step toward him.

"About twenty-four hours."

All of a sudden, Marcus was standing next to her. He wasn't looking at her, though. He was looking behind her. Turning around, she saw two more men approaching. It wasn't the same two as before, though. She squinted into the darkness.

"Jase?" she said quietly.

"Yeah, it's me. Stetson and I heard fighting. What are you

doing so close to the dump, Jessica?" He frowned. "It's way too dangerous for you here."

Jessica sighed. "Two other guys herded me over this way."

"Barnum and Alleman," Marcus said.

Jessica touched his arm. Tension wound through his muscles.

But he was alive. She'd been so worried. Now that he was all right, she wanted nothing more than to find a quiet place to hold him and let him hold her, so they could reassure each other they were all right.

For just a little while, she'd love to believe the lie that everything was okay and they'd be together forever.

20

Marcus tried to project calm, but inside of him, his wolf was going crazy. He would fight for dominance to protect Jessica every night of his damn life, but what would happen to her if he lost?

He had to get her out. No question. No waiting. There was nowhere to hide her, now that they knew she was here. Assholes like Barnum and Alleman would tear the place apart looking for her. They'd come back with help—they had said it themselves, they had been sneaking her into the dump so they wouldn't have to share her. Now that they knew she wasn't easy prey, they might bring others with them next time.

Either way, they sure as hell wouldn't rest until they had a shot at Jessica.

Marcus would die first.

"Easy there," Stetson said.

"What?" Marcus asked.

Stetson shrugged. "I can see all those thoughts going through your head. Try to relax. The answer's not so hard."

Jessica gaped at Stetson.

"Apologies, Miss," Stetson said. "I'm Stetson."

"I'm Jessica."

"Do you have a keen interest in plants?" Stetson asked her, his lip twitching.

Marcus glowered at him.

"I do," she said in surprise.

Marcus took her hand in his. "I got those books for you from Stetson. I think he has a whole library tucked away in his den."

Jessica nodded in understanding.

"A couple of us were talking," Jase said. "Something about mates being able to get across the boundary. Like Carter and Lena. Caitlyn and Grant, too. Seems a mighty strange thing that any of them got out, and especially interesting that they're all couples."

Marcus could guess where this was going, but he kept quiet.

Jase continued, "Have you two tried getting across the line together?"

Jessica shook her head, but Marcus said, "Yes."

Jessica looked up at him in surprise.

"I doubt you noticed," Marcus said to her, "but I tried getting you over the line that very first morning. I held your hand when you touched the wall. I hoped you wouldn't feel anything, and that you'd walk right through the boundary. But it didn't work."

"Maybe you should try it now," Jase suggested.

Jessica shook her head. "I'm not leaving Blythe."

"And how much good will you do her if assholes like Barnum and Alleman capture you?" Marcus asked, anger building within him. "Will it help her be any safer? Will it help her escape? Will it make her feel better to know that you're stuck, too? Will she appreciate your valor that you remain caught in a trap?"

Marcus knew his anger was mostly about Jessica being stuck, but it was also partly about himself. He had saved Marianne, sure, but now he was stuck in here and unable to help her. He could only hope that nobody else came after her like Vince had done.

Jessica took a step back from him and folded her arms over her chest. "And how good would she feel knowing that I just took off as soon as I could? My basic understanding is that she's been abandoned by every person in her life. What kind of friend would I be if I abandoned her, too?"

"A smart one," Stetson said before Marcus could answer her.

"If you can make yourself safe," Jase said, "then the rest of us can worry about saving your friend. We can put all of our efforts into that, rather than dividing our efforts between keeping you safe, and rescuing her."

Marcus's frustration eased. Jase's argument seemed to make sense to Jessica, because she dropped her arms to her sides.

"How do I know that you three won't abandon her like I would be doing?" she asked. "I'm the only person in here who actually knows her and cares about her."

Marcus took one of her hands in his. "I care about you. And if you care about her, then I do, too. Even when she hits me with pipes."

Jase chuckled. "Some of us are calling her Pipe Dreams."

"Like as a nickname?" Jessica asked, wrinkling her nose.

"Exactly that," Jase answered.

Squeezing Jessica's fingers, Marcus said, "Please. Let's try to get you out of here. When you're safe, we can focus on Blythe."

She sent a nervous look at Jase and Stetson, then quietly she said to Marcus, "Do you really think I'm your mate? I mean, I don't know how this works."

"In my pride, all it takes is saying so," Jase said. "I mean, from what I hear, it's a feeling. Both people feel it, and they know. And that's all there is to it."

"Couples exchange mate marks in my pride," Stetson said.

"Mate marks?" Jessica asked.

Before Marcus could close down that conversation, Stetson said, "One or both partners bites the other."

Jase waggled his eyebrows. "During sex."

Jessica's eyes got big and her lips parted. "Like, hard?"

Stetson shrugged.

Jase said, "Hard enough."

Marcus needed to shut this down. Tugging Jessica's hand to get her attention, he said, "Not every mated pair in my pack exchanges mate marks. They aren't considered a necessity. It depends on the couple."

How many times, during sex, had he wanted to mark Jessica? Answer: many. But he had held himself back, because claiming her was wrong. If he couldn't give her a forever, then he had no right claiming it.

"Before anybody bites anybody," Jase said, "maybe you two should just try to walk across one more time?"

Yes, that. That made so much more sense. He led Jessica in the direction of the boundary. "Come on, let's try this."

She dug in her heels. "I should at least tell Blythe what's going on."

"Too dangerous," Jase said.

Marcus was glad it wasn't him always telling her no.

"But I'll pass on the message," Jase added.

Frowning, Jessica went along with Marcus to the gravel

line. Marcus would step over it with her and then come back. And it would work this time, because they'd had sex. The mate magic, or whatever the hell it was, should've worked by now. That first morning, they had barely known each other. He had liked her, and he had wanted her, but he hadn't known her. Now he did.

He was going to miss her. This would hurt like hell.

What was the old line? If you love something, set it free? Well, that's what he was doing now. Even if it broke his fucking heart.

He was vaguely aware of Jase and Stetson watching from a few yards away, but his focus was on Jessica. Her heart beat faster, and her flowery scent was tinged with a faint sourness of anxiety.

He gave her hand a reassuring squeeze. "We can do this. I promise I'll take care of Blythe."

She nodded and gave him a weak smile.

Marcus held out his free arm. If this wasn't going to work, he didn't want to bang his face into a wall. Mirroring him, Jessica held out her free hand. Together, they took a step.

And walked into something solid.

Jessica's shoulders fell. Marcus felt the same disappointment, only his disappointment was tinged with panic. How could he possibly protect her? Even if he had an entire pack working with him, the onslaught of shifters would never end. Even if Barnum and Alleman and anyone else who posed a problem were killed, new shifters arrived in the Junkyard all the time.

He turned back to face Jase and Stetson. Jase shrugged, and Stetson just stared.

"From the outsider's perspective, it seems to me you two are mates," Jase said. "I don't know why this didn't work."

Jessica spoke up. "Maybe he needs to bite me."

"Out of the question," Marcus said at the same time Stetson said, "It's worth a try."

Marcus glared at Stetson.

"Why don't you want to bite me?" Jessica asked. "It seems like it's our last chance for you to get rid of me."

From the tone of her voice, he could tell that her feelings were hurt. He didn't want to get rid of her. He never wanted to let her go. But keeping her here was only putting her in danger.

"I'm not sure what to do," Marcus said. "I don't want to get rid of you, Jessica. But it isn't safe for you here."

"Tell me more about mate marks," she said, her voice firm. She would not take no for an answer, it seemed.

"I already told you when it happens," Jase said.

"Right." Jessica sighed. "But what do they mean? Other than people being mates?"

"In my old pride, that's what they meant." Stetson touched the fourth finger of his left hand, like he was looking for a wedding ring. "They're like a marriage to shifters."

Jessica raised her eyebrows. "Okay."

Jase spoke next. "It seems you two have something to discuss. We'll leave you to it."

He and Stetson walked away.

Marcus and Jessica returned to the trailer, neither of them speaking as they walked. His chest ached. He was fucked either way. Either she left and he lost her, or she stayed and he lost her. He would die trying to protect her, but eventually that was what would happen—he would die. And then who would keep her safe? Nobody else loved her like he did.

Because that's what this was for him—love.

Jessica stopped in front of the trailer door. With her gaze on the ground, she said, "If you don't want to be my mate, you can just say so, right?"

"I'm not sure what you're asking, but it isn't as easy as saying so, one way or the other. For shifters, it's more up to fate than anything else."

"Fuck fate," she said. "I know who I want, and that's you, Marcus."

The conviction in her voice took his breath away. She was stunning—this beautiful, smart woman. He gathered her in his arms and kissed her lips, her chin, her cheeks, her ear, down to her neck. There, on the slope of skin where her neck met her shoulder, he lingered. She tasted like sweet flowers and nature. She tasted like home, love, joy. He was addicted—he would never get enough. His inner wolf gave a low growl of need.

Unlatching the trailer door, he walked inside with her. They stripped off their clothes, and he watched Jessica, her fierce gaze, her feminine curves, the stubborn tilt of her jaw.

"So where do you bite me?" she asked.

He reached out with his hand to touch her collar bone, tracing the ridge to the roundness of her shoulder. "Somewhere along here."

They were completely naked, standing before each other with no barrier, vulnerable. And despite that vulnerability, he felt this was the freest they could possibly get in the Junkyard.

"Is there any special way to do it?" she asked. There was no judgment in her tone, no trepidation, just curiosity.

"Not that I know of." He'd thought about it once or twice, but only after meeting Jessica. "Is there some way you want to do it?"

She shook her head, her cheeks turning pink.

"You shy, Jocelyn?"

"Shut up, Malcolm."

There was his woman, the fire of stubborn irritation shining through her eyes.

"Take me from behind," she said.

He nodded, already looking forward to squeezing her hip and ass while he pounded into her from the back. But first he wanted to kiss her face to face, so he did.

She gasped into his mouth, her tongue coming forward immediately to meet his, her hands grabbing onto his shoulders.

He brought his hand down her neck to her chest, lightly, reverently running his thumb and fingers over her nipples. He licked and kissed her neck, that sweet, tempting place where he would leave his mark.

"Do you really want this?" he asked. "If I do it right, it'll leave a scar."

"Yes," she said. "I want it. I want you."

He could hear her honesty, and her trust in him was as sweet and tantalizing as her flowery scent.

When she began to writhe against him, her body requesting more than his teasing touches on her nipples, he spun her around so she faced the wall. Then he yanked her hips back slightly so her gorgeous ass stuck out. After putting on a condom, he smoothed his hand over her curves. Reaching between her legs, he ran a finger between her lips, testing her readiness for him.

She was soaked.

"Marcus, please," she said, pressing her ass out toward him.

"If you change your mind at any time," he said, rubbing his dick along her pussy, "you say so and we stop immediately. Or we can just fuck, I don't have to bite you. Whatever you want."

"I want this," she said, reaching back to grip his forearm.

So he guided his cock into the sweet, wet heaven of her pussy.

21

Jessica's back arched with desire. The sensation of being filled by Marcus was incomparable to anything else. As he moved within her, the pleasure only built. He smoothed his hand over her back, then brought it to her front, where he cupped one of her breasts and lightly pinched the nipple. She rocked her hips to increase the friction of where they joined, then reached down to touch her clit.

He leaned over her, his chest over her back. She was warm, cherished. For how long, she didn't know, but she would wring every drop of pleasure from this that she could find.

"Bite me, Marcus," she said. "Do it—I'm close."

She felt his lips caress the slope of her shoulder, then his teeth grazed the spot, sharp and scraping. Her body felt ripe and heavy, ready for the ecstasy and the accompanying pain.

He bit down. The sharp sting traveled like a current down her torso, straight to her pussy. She came hard, her legs tensing, her center tightening around Marcus, who thrust a few more times inside of her before he, too, tensed up and squeezed her body to him.

The squeezing pressure of his embrace was exactly what she needed. It felt like he couldn't let her go, and she would be held this way forever.

His mouth was still clamped on her shoulder. He loosened his grip suddenly, with his teeth and with his arms. Then he pulled out of her and spun her around.

"Are you okay?" he asked.

She touched the aching place on her shoulder, and blood smeared. "Um, I guess?"

"Just a second," he said, grabbing a paper towel from the counter and bringing it to the wound. He held it to the bleeding, his eyes intent on Jessica's face.

Looking away, she said, "Really, Marcus, it's fine."

"I shouldn't have done it."

"Fuck that," she said, poking his naked shoulder. "I wanted this mark. Even if it doesn't work. So there."

He grinned and bent to kiss her lips. She sighed into his mouth, her irritation forgotten. But in its place was an unspeakable sorrow. This bite wasn't a symbol of his love, but a symbol of how badly he wanted to get rid of her.

"Well," she said, forcing a brightness into her voice, "I guess we should go test this out, huh?"

He stopped wiping the mark on her shoulder and tilted her chin up so he could look into her eyes.

"I guess we should," he said carefully.

What wasn't he saying?

But instead of asking, she put on her clothes and left the trailer. Morning was approaching, a new lightness in the sky that she could barely see against the branches of the pines and fir. The air was cold against her skin, making her glad she'd opted for a sweatshirt. She kept both the sweatshirt and her t-shirt pulled slightly away from the bite on her shoulder. The bleeding had stopped, but she didn't want the fabric to irritate the wound.

She didn't think anything could compare to the pain she was feeling. Not the pain from her bite—that didn't bother her in the slightest. But the pain of thinking that Marcus didn't want her. The pain of leaving him behind. It didn't feel right, this idea of leaving him here while she was whisked off to safety.

And then there was the notion of him not wanting to bite her. He didn't want to mark her as his. Oh, he had seemed to enjoy it enough. They both had. But now that the post-sex haze had faded, she sensed he was regretting all of it.

Well, screw him, she thought as they walked to the gravel line. He could regret whatever he wanted, but she wasn't going to regret a thing. The only thing she regretted was leaving him.

Then again, she wasn't leaving entirely. If Grant and Caitlyn didn't want to take her in, she'd find a spot to camp out while she waited for Blythe to get free.

Marcus reached for her. Very carefully, he moved her hair aside, uncovering her bite. "Does it hurt?"

"Not really." It stung a little, and it was sore, but she didn't mind it.

"I'm sorry it had to come to that," he said.

Closing her eyes, she inhaled and exhaled slowly. She didn't want to hear anything else about his regret, she didn't want any apologies. She wanted him to hold her tight, so tight like he would never let her go, like he had in the trailer.

They faced the gravel line. As the sky lightened, she could see more of the forest, Caitlyn and Grant's cabin with its darkened windows, and even the outline of the dusky mountains in the distance.

Their toes touched the gravel.

"Well, I guess this is it," Jessica said. "The moment of truth."

"I'm going to miss you," he said.

"No you won't," she said with forced cheer. "I'm not going anywhere until we get Blythe out."

He nodded. "That's right. I forgot."

Her heart felt heavy as a stone. It was like he wanted her to disappear, like he never wanted to see her again. She wasn't sure how to reconcile that with the man who'd just made passionate love to her in the trailer.

She was tired of thinking about it, anyway. Maybe, with a little distance between them, she could start to figure things out.

"All right," Jessica said. "Let's do this."

As before, they held out their free arms. Their other hands were joined.

As before, Jessica felt a solid barrier in front of her.

Startled, she looked up at Marcus. Her feelings were a jumble. Elation, that she wasn't leaving his side after all. Heartache, that they weren't actually mates. She hated the stupid wall. She hated what it was doing to her. It was ridiculous that something invisible could have so much power over her. Not only power over her physically, but power over her emotions. If this was the real world, the world she had grown up in, she would go after Marcus no matter what. There'd be no stupid wall to worry about, no mate marks, no psycho animals trying to get her.

She kicked the wall. "I hate this place!"

When she tried to kick the wall again, Marcus wrapped his arms around her and hauled her back.

"You're going to hurt yourself," he said.

"I don't care. I am just *so mad*."

He didn't say anything; he merely held her tight. Her ear was pressed up against his chest, and she listened to his heartbeat. Instead of calming her, the sound reminded her of what she could not have—Marcus's heart.

"I need to be alone," she said. "I promise to stop kicking the wall."

"Are you sure? I don't want to leave you alone when you're upset."

"I'm sure. Please, get out of here." Her throat choked up on the last words. She didn't want him to see her crying.

His mouth twisted in concern. He looked torn between giving her what she wanted and ignoring her wishes.

"Please," she said. "I'm not asking to run off into the woods like last time. I'll stay in the trailer. I just need space."

"I'll go find Jase or Stetson to keep watch," he said finally, his forehead wrinkled in a frown. "I'm sorry, Jessica."

She wished he would call her by some other name, inject a little levity into the situation, but if she was being real, she knew that their wacky terms of endearment would only make her cry.

Marcus eventually released her. "Are you really sure you want to be alone?"

"Yes." She knew he'd hear the truth.

Sighing, he said, "Okay, if that's what you want."

She couldn't bring herself to look at him, and waited until his footsteps faded away before she went inside the trailer.

Only then did she let her tears fall.

She didn't know how much time passed before a quiet knock came on the trailer door.

"It's Jase. Marcus asked me to come. I'll give you your privacy, but if you need anything, let me know."

"Thanks," she said.

She waited until his footsteps faded away. He'd be able to hear everything she did in here, so she forced herself to breathe past the tightness in her throat until the urge to sob passed.

Then she punched the shit out of one of the pillows.

She was no longer mad at Marcus. She was mad at herself, for falling in love with him.

22

Marcus's cabin had never felt less like his own. It had been weird enough moving into the place after Carter and Lena left the Junkyard. But it was roomier than the trailer, and he could actually stretch out on the bed. Now, though, nothing felt right. He should be with Jessica. He ached to hold her, to wipe away her tears, to erase her sorrow.

He didn't understand why they couldn't get over the boundary line. Mate mark or no, he knew with certainty that she was his mate.

But maybe he wasn't the one for her? It stood to reason that there could be someone else out there to love her as much as he did. She was the best person he knew. Maybe the fates had chosen someone better for her.

The day passed slowly, every moment a rock filling his heart until he felt too heavy to move. He moved between sitting inside the cabin, to sitting outside, and could go no farther.

The sun was dipping, shadows stretching over the forest floor, and Marcus couldn't sit any longer. She'd had all day to herself. He couldn't leave her alone another second while she was hurting.

He stood up, put on his shoes, and left the cabin.

He hadn't gone five yards before a piercing scream rang out over the dump.

His feet refused to move. Heart in his throat, he played the scream over again in his mind. The tone had been wrong for Jessica—a lower pitch.

It had to have been Blythe.

So instead of running for the trailer to check on Jessica, he ran in the other direction, toward the dump. It was what Jessica would want him to do, despite his urges to first check on his mate.

Because she was his mate. He wasn't asking fate about it —he was telling it to himself. As far as his heart and soul were concerned, Jessica was the one for him.

When he reached the dump, he came upon an alarming sight. He had never seen more than Blythe's head, because she had been hidden away in the old RV. Now, however, he saw her entire wiry form as Barnum led her to a cage.

It took Marcus only a second to take in everything in front of him. Blythe screaming, Barnum's fist clenching the back of her sweatshirt as he pushed her forward, and the cage itself—constructed of scrap wood and metal. Barnum must have made it, probably with Alleman's help.

"Get in there," Barnum growled, giving Blythe another shove. "There's gonna be a fight tonight, and you're the prize."

Marcus strode forward. "Let her go. Now."

"Or what?" Barnum said. "Are you going to fight me for this one, too? That's a bit greedy of you, don't you think?"

"You know that's not what I'm doing," Marcus said. "Let her go. This is wrong."

Barnum shoved Blythe the rest of the way into the cage, then slammed the door shut. He fit a padlock into it, then pushed it closed. "Wrong? There's no wrong here. They dumped us in the Junkyard because *we're* wrong. What the fuck else do you expect me to do in here?"

"I expect you to be better." Marcus took careful, restrained steps forward.

"Fuck you. We're moving the fight up to tonight. The Junkyard's tired of waiting."

This was less than ideal. Marcus had thought there would be more time to prep.

Marcus didn't stop advancing until he was within three feet of Barnum. They stared each other down. Marcus was vaguely aware of Blythe in the cage. He got ready to throw the first punch.

Just as he was about to swing, Blythe shouted, "Marcus! Behind you!"

Her warning came too late. Pain exploded through his head and he went down, face first into the mud.

As he lost consciousness, he heard Barnum say, "Now that bitch will be mine."

23

J essica had spent all day moping in the trailer. At one point, Jase had knocked and let her know he would be sending Stetson along to take his place as guard. Then Stetson had knocked, letting her know he was switching with Jase. She wondered how many days would pass this way. She wondered when Marcus would come back. When she had said she wanted time to think, she hadn't meant days and days.

As far as the actual thinking she was doing, it wasn't helping. Her heart felt bruised and achy. Her eyes felt puffy and sore from crying so much. Even flipping through the plant books didn't give her as much comfort as it should have, because they were a reminder of Marcus.

"Giving someone a book isn't a declaration of love," she muttered angrily to herself.

Now that it was evening, and Marcus still hadn't come back, her despair was quickly turning into anger. He should be here, dammit. They should fight for each other. Like she had said earlier, fuck fate. She wasn't going to let fate determine who she loved. She loved Marcus, that was all there was to it. No, she couldn't explain it. She had no idea why it happened so quickly. Maybe it was a shifter thing. Or maybe, when she knew, she knew.

If Marcus didn't arrive in an hour, she was sending Jase out to get him. As much as she'd like to march into the woods and find him herself, she knew that would be the height of stupidity. She had made enough mistakes in this Junkyard.

The sound of snarling animals broke the peaceful quiet. They were close, maybe a couple hundred feet from the trailer.

Someone had come, and they were fighting with Jase.

Rigid with fear, Jessica dropped to the floor of the trailer to hide. Then she realized how silly that was. There was no hiding from shifters—they'd sniff her out regardless of where she went.

She clambered over to the bed where she'd be able to peek out through the curtains. All she could see was darkness, though. Shadows moved through it, but she couldn't make out shapes, not even what animals were out there.

The fighting was over almost immediately. Jessica held her breath, waiting.

Someone knocked on the trailer door and she jumped up. *Please let it be Jase—please let him have won. Or even better —Marcus.*

"Hello," she said softly.

There was no answer.

"Jase? Is that you?"

A sinking feeling in her gut told her it wasn't Jase.

The door banged open. Instead of Marcus or Jase, she was face to face with Alleman. His red-blond hair was streaked with blood, making it look darker, and his black eyes shone with excitement.

He was *happy*. And that was bad news for her.

Immediately, she grabbed the closest thing she had to a weapon—the kitchen knife she had used for slicing apples.

He laughed when he saw her pick it up.

"Barnum, come see," he called over his shoulder. "Our little bitch has a weapon."

A second guy showed up in the doorway. His brown hair was short and his hazel eyes looked dead. He smiled, too, and with those dead eyes, his smile was just as creepy as Alleman's. "The pup has claws."

Holding the knife out in front of her, Jessica tried to steady her breathing. Her arm was shaking wildly, but she would not hesitate to cut one of these guys—or better, both. They might win the fight, but she wasn't going down easy.

Alleman looked from the knife to her face and laughed again. Then he lunged toward her.

A week ago, Jessica would not have been able to even track his movements. But after spending all day, every day with Marcus, she had more of a fighting chance. She slashed out with the knife, and what she lacked in confidence, she made up for with panic.

The knife wasn't very sharp, but it sliced through Alleman's forearm anyway. She must've caught him somewhere important, because he was bleeding a lot.

"You'll pay for that," he growled, before reaching for her again.

She slashed out with the knife again, but she wasn't as lucky this time. The blade merely grazed the top of his hand, and then his arms were reaching around her in a chilling mockery of an embrace. He squeezed her wrist until she was forced to drop the knife.

She stomped on his foot, but she wasn't wearing shoes and he was, and it probably hurt her heel more than it hurt him. She used her elbows, knees, and feet, trying to get free. He merely grunted when she made contact.

"She's a feisty one," he said to Barnum. He lifted her and carried her the few steps toward the door.

Jessica's hand was free, just barely, and she tried to grip the door jamb. She knew the effort was futile. These guys were stronger, bigger, faster.

They left the trailer. Several yards away, a figure was lying on the ground, a huge mountain lion, probably Jase. The big cat wasn't moving, and she was too far away to see if its body rose and fell with breaths.

As Alleman continued carrying her, she tried to scream for Marcus. As soon as a sound left her throat, Alleman's hand came over her mouth. He smelled like beer and body odor. She tried to bite his hand anyway, but he held her face in a way that she couldn't.

He carried her through the dark forest, step after purposeful step. Jessica was facing forward, grateful for at least the smidgen of mercy that she could see where they were headed. One of his arms was banded around her arms and waist, the other he kept over her mouth.

Barnum walked nearby, but not too close. She doubted either of them trusted the other. Maybe she could use that to her advantage. She tried to talk through Alleman's hand, to make it seem as if she was more panicked than usual, and then to signal with her eyes that Barnum was coming after her. But Alleman ignored her.

They reached the dump. Jessica recognized the school bus, then the RV where Blythe was staying. The tractor was still next to it, where she and Marcus had hidden that night when they visited Blythe. But there was a gaping hole in the back of the RV.

Jessica struggled again, harder. Where was Blythe? What had they done with her?

They came around the edge of the RV, and Jessica found Blythe. She sat in a giant cage that looked like it had been constructed from random pieces of metal and fencing. Blythe was sitting with her knees up to her chest, her arms wrapped around them, but she looked up as Jessica and her captors moved closer.

"Jessica!" Blythe shouted.

Barnum fiddled with the lock on the door, then yanked it open. Blythe rushed forward, but Barnum held her back while Alleman pushed Jessica into the cage. The force of Alleman's shove sent Jessica to her knees and she yelped at the sharp sting of pain.

Blythe spit at them as the cage door clanged shut. "Monsters," she hissed.

Barnum shrugged, and Alleman laughed.

"You will each become attached to one of us eventually," Alleman said. "Once you're mated, the others will leave you alone. Doesn't that sound nice?"

"If that's the truth," Jessica shot back, "then I'm already mated."

"That so?" Alleman said.

"Yes, Marcus is my mate."

He gave her a sly grin. "I sense a lie there."

Dammit. She wanted Marcus to be her mate, but the barrier had other ideas. Shouldn't her heart's desire count more than some stupid magic spell?

The two men walked away, Barnum whistling as he went.

Blythe helped Jessica off her knees and into a more comfortable sitting position. Jessica hugged her friend, relieved to see her whole and uninjured.

"I was so worried about you," Jessica said.

Blythe squeezed her tighter. "I was fine until a couple hours ago. They ripped apart my RV and hauled me to this cage. Your guy, Marcus, tried to save me."

Jessica leaned back from Blythe, terror thrumming through her veins. "Marcus? Is he okay?"

"I think so. They knocked him out and dragged him away. But he was still breathing, from what I could see."

"As soon as he wakes up, he'll save us," Jessica said. She knew it with every fiber of her being. Marcus wouldn't rest until she was safe.

The realization was swift and sudden. This was why he wanted her gone, out of the Junkyard. It wasn't because he didn't like her. It wasn't because he didn't think they were mates. It was because he thought her departure was the only way she would be safe. He had said it, but she hadn't really internalized the meaning until this moment. This situation was exactly what he feared.

She understood now.

Not that it would've made any difference, though, not with the boundary keeping them inside.

Jessica stood up. "We need to search the cage for weaknesses. Nobody's around. If we can pull it apart, even just a tiny bit, maybe we can crawl through and escape."

"I've tried it," Blythe said. "Even though it looks like a piece of shit, every bit of wire and metal holds. Besides, if we get out, where are we supposed to run to?"

Jessica grimaced at the ramshackle cage walls. "I don't know, but we're not staying here."

24

M arcus woke to a thudding smack against his cheek. His head rocked sideways, and he blearily opened his eyes.

Standing over him was Jase. He wore a grim expression.

"Is Blythe okay?" Marcus asked, sitting up. As soon as he could stand, he would go again and try to free her.

Jase held out his hand, and Marcus took it. Jase hauled him to his feet.

"It's not just Blythe now," Jase said in a low voice. "They have Jessica, too."

It took a moment for the words to take on meaning, but when they did, Marcus felt his heart tear in two.

"You were supposed to protect her." Marcus couldn't keep the rage from his voice, and he clenched his fist.

Then he took a closer look at Jase. The entire left side of his face was bruised, and his shoulder looked off, like it was dislocated.

"You tried to defend her," Marcus said in understanding.

"Fuckers snuck up on me," Jase said. "We need to get her back."

"Fuck yes we do." Marcus swayed on his feet, but he willed the dizziness away. He had to get to Jessica. She was scared, and she could be hurt.

He took stock of their surroundings. They were close to the boundary, but in the dump area of the junkyard. Barnum, or maybe it was Alleman, had dragged Marcus here after knocking him out. They'd tied him up, too, he realized when he saw the ropes surrounding him. Jase had cut him loose.

Nodding at Jase, he said, "Are both of the women in that cage?"

"I don't know about a cage," Jase said.

"It's why Barnum and Alleman knocked me out. I heard Blythe scream, so I ran out there. They had taken apart the RV to get her, and when I arrived, Barnum was forcing her into a cage. Alleman came up behind me."

"If they're in a cage, they might be safe for now," Jase said.

"But probably not for long," Marcus said. "Barnum and Alleman moved the fight—it's tonight."

"Fuck," Jase said.

Sure enough, as soon as he spoke the words, a roar rose up from the other side of the dump.

He looked at Jase. "It's starting. Let's go."

"We should check it out first," Jase said. "It would be smarter."

Marcus darted forward. "Dammit, I am not about to put the woman I love in danger just so we can be smart about this."

"I'm not asking you to put her in danger." Jase grabbed Marcus's arm. "I'm asking you to keep yourself alive long enough to save her."

Marcus spun around, ready to hit him, but then he

stopped. Underneath his alarm was a rational person, one who could think strategically. He had to be not only strong, but smart.

Nodding at Jase, he said, "Okay. We'll go in from the south, slowly, see who's there, who we're up against. Maybe some of them are like you, and they'll fight just for the women's freedom, not for any twisted sort of claim."

"You have rather high hopes for our ragtag group," Jase said.

Marcus shrugged, remembering something Jessica told him. "Sometimes you have to look past someone's reputation to find out who they really are."

Not waiting for Jase to respond, he moved toward the southern boundary of the Junkyard, the place where their ice chests of food were dropped off each Sunday. His head ached, but at least he could see clearly and he was no longer swaying.

Jase followed a few paces behind him, likely keeping a closer eye out for threats than Marcus was. Marcus could barely be bothered to take in his immediate surroundings—his focus was on one objective—finding Jessica and beating the assholes who'd dared to take her from him.

They reached the fighting ring, which was a dirt circle outlined in old tires. Several guys milled around the ring, and inside of it stood Alleman and Vezirov. Marcus didn't know Vezirov at all, just that he'd come into the Junkyard a week or so after Marcus had. Marcus didn't remember what Vezirov's charges were, so he had no guesses as to whether Vezirov would be an ally or enemy.

More important than the shifters were the two women huddled in a crudely formed cage that sat off to the side of the ring like an afterthought. It was too close to the others for Marcus to even consider sneaking over to it and freeing the women.

Jessica and Blythe sat next to each other, their hands out of sight. As Marcus watched, one of them looked at the ring, then said something, and then the two of them scooted over a foot.

They were trying to break out of the cage without calling attention to themselves. Smart. But hopefully they wouldn't need to break out. Hopefully, Marcus and Jase would fight off everyone who threatened them, and those who would be left would be willing to leave them alone, learn to respect them.

It might be too much to hope for, but hope was all Marcus had at this point.

He took in more details, his focus caressing Jessica's face. Her eyes were wide with fright, but her mouth was set with determination, her chin jutting out with her usual stubbornness.

Tearing his gaze away from Jessica, he looked again at the assembled shifters.

There were three guys he knew for sure would be bad news—Alleman, Barnum, and Buenevista. Vezirov was an unknown. Markowicz was out there, and he seemed okay. Stetson was there, and he was good people. Ephraimson was there, too, with his big, dark blond beard. Marcus was surprised—Ephraimson was a loner like Stetson, not much of a joiner. He usually kept to his truck where he experimented with making moonshine.

So far, the fighting looked to be taking place in a somewhat orderly fashion. Two guys in the ring at once. Marcus guessed that as the night progressed, everyone would start becoming more feral, fighting as beasts instead of men, and the "rules" of the fights would turn into mere suggestions before becoming laughably forgotten.

Didn't matter. He wasn't letting the night progress that far—he would get Jessica out of here long before then.

Vezirov threw a punch at Alleman and connected with Alleman's jaw. Alleman's head snapped back, but Alleman was quick enough on his feet and backed up so he wouldn't fall over. He ducked slightly, lowering his center of balance. Marcus saw it for what it was—a preparation for a leg-sweep, but Vezirov wasn't as experienced. He tried to dodge Alleman's leg, but he didn't quite make it. As soon as he fell, he was up again, a snarl on his lips.

Marcus couldn't be bothered with watching the mechanics of the fight. He was more concerned with calculating his and Jase's chances of success.

"What do you think?" he whispered to Jase. "I run in, and you get anyone you can on our side. Stetson, at least, will be with us."

Jase shrugged. "It doesn't look great for us, but we have a chance if we join the fray at the right time."

"The right time is before Jessica and Blythe can get hurt," Marcus said.

"I don't disagree, but—"

A sick thud filled the air and Vezirov flew back, his head knocking into one of the tires lining the ring. His eyes closed and he lay still. He was breathing, but unconscious.

"I'm the first winner!" Alleman shouted. He leered at the cage, at Blythe and Jessica.

The women sat huddled together, their hands behind them, no doubt working furiously at the metal and wire, searching for weaknesses.

"There are no winners yet," Buenevista said, his eyes flashing with irritation.

"Says who?" Alleman made a lap around the ring, then jumped nimbly over Vezirov's unconscious form.

Several guys booed him.

"Which one of you will be my mate?" he asked, peering into the cage at Blythe and Jessica. "Not sure either of you can open your mouth wide enough to take all of me. Maybe I should hold auditions."

Marcus growled and tensed his legs to spring.

"Wait—" Jase started.

Marcus pulled away and took a flying leap into the ring, both of his arms up, his single fist clenched. Looking Alleman dead in the eye, he said, "I'll kill you before you can even finish opening the cage door."

He vaguely heard Jase behind him saying, "Aw, hell."

25

J essica gasped when Marcus leaped from the shadows. She'd never seen him so full of rage as he was now—his fist poised to strike, his mouth twisted in a snarl, his eyes murderous.

He was here. She knew he'd come, and she knew everything would be all right.

Then again, there were a lot of guys around here. How many would join Marcus and Jase? How many would fight against them, instead? She had no way of knowing.

As she watched, her throat clogged with anxiety, Marcus tackled Alleman to the ground with a roar.

Chaos broke out among the other men, some of them cheering Marcus, some cheering Alleman. Some of them looked as if they'd jump into the ring and join the fight.

Were there rules here? She looked around, trying to see what was stopping those clustered around the tires from wading into the melee. Jase stood nearby, holding up his hand. Thank God he was okay. The last she'd seen him... she'd feared the worst.

Marcus and Alleman rolled together in the dirt. Their

arms and legs were moving so quickly, Jessica could barely tell who was who. The sound of fists hitting flesh repeated in her ears, over and over again like an off-beat rhythm. If she survived this, she feared she'd hear that sound forever in her mind.

Marcus's head flew back. He shook himself, dazed. Alleman continued the assault, not giving Marcus a chance to recover.

But Marcus was holding on. He wasn't giving up. He had something that Alleman didn't have—he had honor, strength. He'd keep fighting, until his dying breath.

Jessica needed to see him survive. "Please, please," she murmured.

"Hey," Blythe nudged her shoulder. "Can you reach the piece of wire I'm holding?"

Jessica had forgotten all about their escape efforts—she'd been too involved in the fighting. Craning her neck to see behind Blythe, she saw the shiny metal of the wire. "I think so."

"Good. Grab it, and hang onto it so I can find the other."

The angle was awkward, but she got her arm behind Blythe and grabbed the wire. "I got it."

Blythe kept her gaze forward, so Jessica did the same. Occasionally, Blythe's fingers brushed Jessica's in her search for the other piece of wire.

"Got it," Blythe whispered. "What do you see back there?"

Jessica pretended to wince at the display of violence in front of her, and she hid her face behind Blythe's shoulder. The shadows made it hard to see, but she could discern the outline of the wires. They'd been twisted together to latch a wide, rusty bar in place.

"If we can unwind them," Jessica said, "we'll free the lower end of this bar."

Blythe tilted her head back, checking out the width of the bar and the space on either side of it. "That still won't be enough space for us to squeeze through."

"No," Jessica said, "it won't. But we could use it as a lever, maybe pry something else loose. It's the best chance we have."

While she and Blythe worked on the wires together, Jessica watched Marcus and Alleman. Her stomach lurched each time Marcus took a hit, but he gave as good as he got. Alleman leaped at him, but Marcus went low, then used his bent knees as a spring to shove Alleman away.

Marcus lifted his head and looked directly at Jessica. Blood dripped from his nose and from the side of his forehead, but his eyes were clear. His intent was clear. He would fight for her, no matter what.

Then he turned toward Jase and the others. Jase's hand was lifted, but Jessica had no idea why. He looked like he was waiting for a teacher to call on him in class.

Marcus raised his voice, shouting, "Now!"

Jase lowered his hand. A few of the surrounding shifters looked confused, like they didn't know what the "now" was about, but more of them sprang into action, grabbing the confused looking guys and holding them back when they could, or throwing punches when they couldn't.

Alleman got up and circled Marcus. He wore a maniacal grin. An angry scar on his neck seemed to pulse with malicious intent. "Come on, One-hand. Show me what you got."

Marcus didn't respond. He didn't even blink.

Jessica felt the end of the wire she'd been working on. "I think we got it untwisted."

Blythe tugged, and so did Jessica. The bar behind them

gave way. It was still attached at the top of the cage, but now it could swing loose.

Nobody was watching them, so Jessica stood, and Blythe followed her lead. Together, they pulled the bar. It had been more weakly attached at the top than the bottom, and they pulled it free.

Jessica's hand was bleeding—she wasn't sure what had done it, the pointy end of the wire, or the sharp edge of the bar. She wiped it on her leg and helped Blythe maneuver the bar to the side, wedging it in between the two bars that had been on either side of this one.

"Push toward the right?" Jessica asked.

"Yeah," Blythe said.

They shoved the free end of the bar and a loud wrenching sound came from the bar adjacent.

"One good kick should do it," Jessica said, glancing over her shoulder. Luckily, all of the guys were too occupied with their mayhem to pay attention to her and Blythe. She kicked hard at the weakened bar, and it sprang free.

She turned back to the violence in front of her, struggling to find Marcus in the brawl. He was on top of Alleman again, holding him down with his right arm while he punched him with his left fist.

But a leopard was approaching from behind them.

"Look out!" Jessica yelled.

Marcus turned just in time to dodge out of the way, scrambling off of Alleman in the process.

Alleman's attention went straight to Jessica. He saw the bars in her and Jessica's arms and shouted, "The women are getting away!"

Someone else said, "Yeah, but where can they go?"

"Good point." Alleman circled around Marcus on one side.

The leopard kept trying to get behind him. Jessica couldn't bear to tear her gaze away. Why was nobody helping Marcus?

"Come on," Blythe said. "We'll find somewhere to hide."

"No, we have to help," Jessica said.

Blythe squeezed through the opening they'd made. "I don't know—"

"Those guys—some of them are fighting to help us. I think we should help them, too."

"You're right." Blythe bent down and picked something up. "Hey, I think this is my pipe."

Jessica squeezed out of the cage while Blythe gave her pipe an experimental swing.

Blythe smiled. "It's the same one. Look, there's a piece of rebar by that tire."

Jessica ran over and grabbed it. "Let's kick some ass."

Hefting her rebar in her hands, Jessica came out of the shadows behind the cage. The scene before them had gotten even more violent and frenzied. The scent of blood filled the air, along with the sounds of growling and thudding fists. Several of the guys had transformed into beasts—there was the leopard, a bear, and a couple of mountain lions and wolves.

Even while she watched, glowing white lights surrounded the remaining men as they shifted into their animal forms.

Marcus faced Alleman. "Let's finish this as beasts."

Alleman nodded. "I can't wait to tear out your throat, wolf."

The two men yanked off their shirts, shoved off their jeans and shoes, and crouched on the ground. But the leopard who'd been circling earlier was not giving Marcus space—he looked like he would leap at Marcus while he was vulnerable.

"Let's get the leopard," Jessica whispered, squeezing Blythe's arm.

Nodding, Blythe inched forward with her. Jessica picked up a dirt clod and threw it as hard as she could. It hit the leopard straight in the back of the head. He turned around, snarling. Jessica knew he'd be fast, so as soon as he darted toward them, she started swinging. Blythe did the same.

There was a cracking sound as Jessica's rebar made contact with the leopard's head, and Blythe hit him a second later. He went down hard, and lay unmoving.

Shit, had they *killed* him? She nudged him with the end of her rebar, and he growled before his eyes rolled back into his head. Staring hard at his fur, she waited until she could see him breathing.

"He's alive," Blythe said.

Jessica stood taller, looking for her next opponent. But the gray wolf in the ring, Marcus, had his jaws locked on the throat of Alleman's mountain lion.

Alleman kicked, but Marcus only held him more tightly. Alleman went still, his eyes rolling angrily. Marcus clamped down even more. The stench of blood filled Jessica's nostrils —Alleman's, Marcus's, and everyone else's, she guessed.

Finally, Alleman growled and lowered his gaze.

It didn't look to Jessica like a motion of submission that would last forever, but it would last for now, at least. Marcus let him go but stood over him.

A white light surrounded the mountain lion. Once it faded, Marcus's gray wolf was standing over Alleman, naked and bloodied.

"Yes, I concede, dammit," Alleman said, his voice a growl. "I won't attack. Fuck."

Marcus shifted back into his wolf. He turned to face everyone—all of them bloody, most of them naked after shifting back to human. Jessica kept her gaze on Marcus as he spoke.

"We're *not* monsters. Doesn't matter who dumped us in the Junkyard or why. If a woman is not willing, that is the *end* of your pursuit. Jessica is my mate, and Blythe is a friend. You will stay away from them both."

"Fuck you," Alleman said in a raspy voice, through his injured throat.

"If you can't respect it, you won't live here," Jase said, standing tall. "We will end you, put you down."

Alleman spit on the ground, but his shoulders slumped.

"We're not fighting about this every damn night," Marcus said. "You're either going to fall in line and respect a woman's right to consent, or you die. We don't have anywhere else to throw you. So what's it going to be?"

Barnum, the leopard at Jessica's feet, stirred, then shifted back to human. He sat up. "The fuck's going on?"

"We lost," Alleman said. "Let's go."

There was grumbling from some, but the crowd thinned out. Injured shifters walked gingerly or limped away, back to wherever they made their beds. Soon, it was only Marcus, Jase, Blythe, and Jessica. Marcus and Jase found their clothes on the ground. They dressed and came toward the women.

The sun was beginning to rise, its early gray light sneaking through the trees and clouds. The nightmare was finally over.

Jessica stumbled toward Marcus, relief making her knees weak. "I'm so glad you're okay," she whispered.

Marcus gathered her in his arms. "I've never been more

scared in my life," he said, "as I was when I found out they'd taken you."

"Did you really mean what you said about me being your mate?" Jessica asked.

"Yes. I don't care what the boundary does to us." Marcus squeezed her tightly. "It can keep us in, let us out, it doesn't matter. You're my mate, and I'm yours."

26

M arcus kept his arms around Jessica. Her freesia scent filled his nose. Over anything else, her happy, sweet scent was a reassurance to him that she was all right. There was something coppery mixed with it, though.

"You smell like blood," he said.

"There's a cut on my hand, from the cage. It isn't bad."

He picked up her hand, needing to see for himself. She wasn't a shifter; she wouldn't heal like he would.

A teasing smile graced her lips when he turned to gaze at her again. "I told you it isn't bad. Couldn't you hear that I was telling the truth?"

"I can't help it." He tugged her close again. "I have to make sure you're okay."

He was aware of Blythe and Jase standing nearby, but he was having a hard time letting Jessica go.

"Sorry, for my part in all of this," Jase said, his dual colored eyes—one gold, one green—lowered in regret. "They took me down. If they hadn't surprised me, Jessica, you wouldn't have been brought to the cage."

"It's okay," Jessica said, giving Jase a gentle smile. "It all worked out."

"It's nearly impossible to keep someone safe here," Marcus added.

Jase pointed to the gravel line nearby. "You two should try again."

Frowning, Marcus stared at the boundary. They'd tried twice. He didn't know why it hadn't worked, and he hardly cared. He knew Jessica was his mate, without a doubt. They might have to figure out how to stay safe here in the Junkyard for the rest of their lives, despite whatever other shifters got dumped here, despite the grumbling acceptance he'd received from the others after he and Jase had laid down the law.

Jessica pulled out of Marcus's embrace. She took the few steps over to Blythe and grabbed Blythe's hand. Her eyes glistened with tears as she looked at Marcus. "I'm sorry—I can't leave without Blythe. I know I said I'd do it earlier, but there's just no way."

Marcus was about to respond, but Blythe let go of Jessica's hand and spun to face her.

"Are you shitting me?" Blythe asked, her green eyes narrowed. "If you have a chance, you need to get out. I'll be pissed if you stay for me. I'll tie you up and push you over the line if I have to."

Marcus tended to agree with her.

"But I'm part of the reason you're in here," Jessica said. "If I hadn't gotten you in trouble—"

Blythe interrupted her. "We both know Chaole was looking for a reason to boot me from the program. It's okay, Jessica. I'll find my own way out. Jase told me there's a witch or something."

"The witch died," Jessica said.

"Then we'll find another fucking witch," Blythe said in an exasperated tone. "If you can get out, I want you out. And you'll come visit me, I hope?"

"Of course," Jessica said.

"Good." Blythe hugged her.

"But I'm not going without Marcus," Jessica said.

Marcus took her hand. "Like I'd let you get away from me."

"Really?" She looked up at him, hope shining in her brown eyes. "You'll leave with me?"

When he nodded, she flashed him a brilliant smile. Then she looked once more at Blythe. "If you're sure…"

"Yes. Go. Right now." Blythe grinned.

"She's not lying to me, is she?" Jessica stage-whispered to Marcus.

"Hey," Blythe said, affronted.

Laughing, Marcus led Jessica forward. "She's telling the truth. She wants you to go."

"Just had to make sure," Jessica said over her shoulder. Pointing at Marcus and then at Jase, she said, "Look out, they're lie detectors."

Marcus and Jessica were three feet from the gravel. Three feet from freedom. Marcus didn't know why he thought it would work now, when it hadn't before, other than a feeling of rightness in his gut. Maybe a person had to be free on the inside before they could be free on the outside.

The sun had fully risen. Dawn's gray light brightened into a rosy morning, and birds called to each other from their perches. Two chipmunks chased each other around a pile of rusted hubcaps.

"Ready?" he asked her.

"With you, always."

They held hands. Their third attempt. He held his breath, pushed out with his free arm, and they each took a giant step over the gravel.

Nothing stopped them.

Jessica squeezed his hand, and he squeezed hers back. His feet were bare because he hadn't bothered putting on shoes after the fight. He was glad, though, because there was nothing between his soles and the earth outside the Junkyard.

Looking down at Jessica, he couldn't help but smile when he saw the excited grin on her face.

"I knew it," he said.

"We never should have doubted," she answered.

"Damn right." He bent his head to hers and kissed her, hard and sweet.

"You fucking did it!" Blythe whooped.

Marcus and Jessica turned around to face the other two. Blythe was bouncing on the balls of her feet and smiling hard. She rushed to the gravel line and placed her hands up against the wall—there was no give.

"It's freaking magic," she said. "I can't believe you two got over!"

Jase wore a small smile as well, but he wasn't looking at Marcus and Jessica—he was looking at Blythe.

"Do you see that?" Marcus said, loud enough only for Jessica's ears.

"I do," she muttered from the corner of her mouth. In a louder voice, addressing Blythe and Jase, she said, "I have an idea. The guys in there sounded more agreeable to the mate argument Marcus posed. It's a long shot, but Blythe and Jase, you could say you're mates, and Blythe could be better protected by that."

"Except," Marcus said, "we can sense lies."

Yet, the way Jase was looking at Blythe, with a soft look in his eyes...maybe it would work.

But the way Blythe was looking at Jase right now, with surprise and disgust on her face...definitely not.

"Not all mates are madly in love," Marcus said. "In my pack, half the time it was more about commitment than it was about fate."

"Just something to think about," Jessica added, smirking at Blythe.

Rolling her eyes, Blythe said, "Yeah, I'll think about it."

"That was a lie," Marcus said, grinning.

"Fine, be stubborn," Jessica said to Blythe. "But at the very least, you should move into the trailer. The rest of the tequila is still with my backpack in there. Speaking of— would you mind getting the backpack for me? And the books, and a notebook?"

"I'll bring you your backpack and books," Blythe said. "But I'm keeping the tequila."

Jessica laughed. "Fair enough."

Blythe stopped ten feet away. "Um, where's the trailer?"

"I'll take you there." Jase said quickly. He nodded at Marcus and Jessica, then jogged to Blythe's side.

"He's a goner," Marcus said, pulling Jessica into his arms again and resting his chin on the top of her head.

Wrapping her arms around him, Jessica asked, "Do you think so?"

"Yeah. The way he's looking at her? Like the world revolves around her? That's how I feel about you, Josephine."

"I feel the same about you, Marvin. And look how much bigger our revolving world just became. You're free now. *We're* free."

"Yeah, I guess we are. But it wouldn't mean anything to me if we weren't together."

"I agree one hundred percent," she said. "But now I'm wondering...what's next?"

"This." He bent to kiss her again, his lips meeting hers in a gentle, probing heat.

And whatever else was to come? He could picture it clearly in his mind. A little house for them to live in, with a greenhouse in the back filled with lots of plants for her to study. A forest behind that, where he could run. Days spent laughing together, learning more about each other. Nights spent eliciting pleasure from each other's bodies and sleeping in warm embraces.

Together. Free.

27

J essica frowned at the index card in front of her. On it, she had taped a print-out of a plant drawing. The scientific name for the plant was on the tip of her tongue. All she'd have to do was flip around the card and she'd see it.

"Come on," she muttered. "I know you..."

She knew dozens of scientific names, including all of those of the plants she had used to decorate her and Marcus's little rental home.

Yes, it was a rental. Her parents had offered to buy them a house, but Jessica wanted to do things on her own—and Marcus had agreed. She loved her parents, but their favors often came with expectations, and she didn't want to have to worry about their expectations anymore. She had her own goals and dreams.

So she was getting a second degree in botany, and she had a part-time job with the forestry service. Marcus had found work designing websites, much to Jessica's surprise. She hadn't known he was a tech-head, but apparently he had a real talent for it.

Marcus came in the back door, naked, a pair of sweat-pants balled up in his hand.

She loved it when he came back fresh from a run in the woods. He smelled like trees and earth, and he was always naked, with his short hair sticking up at wild angles. It made her want to press her body to his and run her fingers through his hair.

"Can you take a break?" he asked.

"Mm, yeah. The quiz isn't until next week." The community college course was low stakes, but she wanted to do well on it. She loved studying botany and she was getting clearer on what she'd do with that passion—teach others about plants, as well, and how important they were to ecosystems.

Her parents were still trying to understand Jessica's dream. Jessica was learning, though, that whether or not they understood was their business, and not Jessica's. Spending time in the Junkyard with Marcus had taught her that sometimes things were out of your control, and you had to take your own path to the best of your ability and let others take theirs.

Like Blythe, opting to stay behind. Jessica had spoken to her last week, and she was doing well. Jase had stood several yards away, in the trees, and Blythe told Jessica she could barely walk ten steps without him shadowing her.

Marcus placed his hand on Jessica's shoulder, and warmth spread through her body.

"You want some help studying?" he asked.

"No, I think I'm done for the night." She flipped over the index card and read the plant name, committing it to memory. Then she looked up at Marcus. "Are you excited about Marianne coming for dinner?"

He nodded. "She's bringing someone, did I tell you?"

"No, you didn't. Friend, or something more?"

He scowled. "Something more."

"Be nice," Jessica said, leaning back into the couch. "Marianne deserves love and she's smart enough to weed out the duds."

"I guess you're right," Marcus said.

She straightened her index cards. "I'm always right."

"You know, I saw this in my head. Exactly like this."

"What?" She tossed her notebook and index cards on the coffee table. "Me tearing my hair out trying to memorize more scientific names?"

He laughed, then flopped down on the sofa next to her. "No. I saw you and me, in a little house like this one. Filled with plants."

She looked around at the cluttered windowsills and counters, at the several pots on the coffee table and the hanging plants in the kitchen. "There aren't that many plants, come on."

"Judi, there is no end to the plants in this house."

"There's plenty of room for more," she said, sniffing and leaning forward to grab her notebook.

"Yeah?" he asked. "Where?"

"In your pants." She pretended to read the words on the page in front of her, but she was more attuned to Marcus's heat. "Plenty of room in your pants."

He went still, and his voice was low when he said, "Juliet, are you talking about the size of my cock?"

"Not at all, Macaulay. Why would I do that?" She looked over and gave him a big grin, and saw the playfulness sparkling in his eyes.

"Maybe you miss it. It's already been...what, six or seven hours since I gave you orgasms." Marcus reached for her.

She shrieked, trying to scoot to the other side of the couch, but he caught her around the waist and tugged her into his lap. Snuggling into him, she breathed deeply, inhaling the scent of the forest on his skin. The cock in question was half-hard and pinned between her hip and his stomach. She wiggled, giving herself enough room to reach down and stroke his generous length.

She could try to make fun of his cock all she wanted, but he'd hear the truth in the end—she was damn impressed by it, by the way it filled her and wrung every drop of pleasure from her body. His dick should be the model manufacturers used to make sex toys.

Kissing the side of her neck, Marcus whispered, "Do you want more orgasms, Jessica?"

Ooh, he was using her name. Play-fighting time was over, and her panties were already getting damp.

She moaned in response to his question, then pulled off her shirt.

His hand immediately went to her breasts, where he alternated light strokes with harder pinches, working her into a frenzy on his lap.

Now that she was on the pill, she could take him bare, and she loved that freedom, to be able to fuck whenever and wherever they felt like it. She shoved him so he reclined against the back of the couch, climbed off his lap, then took off her shorts and panties.

"Jessica," he said in wonder. "I will never get tired of this view."

Easing down over him, she straddled his thighs and watched in approval as he held up his cock so she could impale herself on it.

"Marcus," she gasped as she eased down.

He kissed her, his tongue asking entrance to her mouth. She granted it, twining her tongue with his as she slowly lowered the rest of the way onto him, allowing her body to stretch around his girth. So thick, so good.

He held her neck with his arm, keeping her in place for his kiss. With his hand, he lightly pinched her nipples. She felt drenched with slippery wetness as she glided over him, lifting up and down to take pleasure and to give it. A light sheen of sweat decorated his chest and she ran her fingers over him, delighting in the signs of their exertion.

Her orgasm was building, filling her body, causing her muscles to tense. She rocked harder against him, changing the angle so her clit would drag against him.

"Marcus," she whispered against his mouth.

Their kiss grew frantic along with the rolling movement of her hips, and pleasure sparked throughout her body. She shouted with her release.

Marcus let go of her neck and breasts to grab her hips and thrust up into her, drawing out her aftershocks while he chased his own orgasm. He came, the heat of his come coating her inside.

"I love you, Jessica," he said, reaching up to tuck a strand of her hair behind her ear.

She squeezed her walls around him, and grinned when she felt him twitch.

"Greedy woman—you want more already?" he asked.

"With you? Always." She winked and squeezed him again.

Grabbing her around the waist, he pressed her down and over the couch, then hovered over her, gazing at her with his beautiful gray eyes.

"We have all evening and into the night," he said. "Tell me what you want to do first."

She had a few million ideas, but she knew they'd get to

them all eventually. There was no rush, no danger. They had all night in this little house, and years and years after this.

Ready for more trashy romance? Pick up *Filthy Alpha*, the next book in the series!

"So, we need to fuck," Blythe said, walking into Jase's workshop.

Jase dropped the metal piece he'd been holding, which he'd been getting ready to screw into the waiting table top perched against the sawhorses.

"What?" he asked.

Hell, he was down, but she couldn't have actually meant what she said.

"Have intercourse." Her tone was patient but businesslike. "Sex. Make love. Screw. Do each other. Make some hanky panky—"

"I got it." He stared at her, at the way her flame-red hair framed her face and made her green eyes shine. *Make some hanky panky.* Had she really just said that? "I just don't understand where this sudden desire to *jump my bones* has come from."

She was already lifting her shirt over her head, revealing her tits. Fuck, she wasn't even wearing a bra. His dick leapt to attention.

"Barnum was asking questions," she said simply, her green eyes blazing as she dropped her shirt on the floor. She took several steps toward Jase. "If he figures out we're supposed mates who aren't even fucking, I won't be protected here any longer."

Her breasts were smaller than a handful, and her nipples were a soft shade of pink against her creamy skin, which was lightly freckled.

She stopped in front of him. Her tits were eye level. He salivated, swallowed, longing to take one of those hardened nipples into his mouth. Did she have any idea what kind of effect she had on him?

"I can give you head, first," she offered, "if you're not in the mood."

"You—you mean right now?" He was half-ready to rip off his pants. Then he stopped, clenched his fists on his thighs. "No. Stop it, Blythe."

"Why? Don't you want me?"

He was thankful as fuck that humans couldn't sense dishonesty, because there was only one thing he could tell her that would convince her to drop this nonsense. "No, I'm not interested."

She huffed a sigh of exasperation. "Why the hell not? I'm assuming you haven't gotten laid in a long while. I know I don't have a lot to offer in the curves department, but I'm sure fucking me would be better than jacking off."

"It's not that," he said, swallowing again. "It complicates things. We're mates, and that should be good enough for all the guys here."

Frowning, she marched back to where she'd dropped her shirt. Every cell in his body screamed *no* as she put it back on, hiding her gorgeous body once more. That shirt was a crime against humanity.

"I disagree," she said. "But I'm not going to beg. If you change your mind, let me know. I'll be at our cabin, writing."

She walked out of his workshop, her tight little ass swaying gently in those jeans, and he groaned aloud.

He wanted nothing more than to rip off her clothes, bend her over the smooth metal he'd perched on the sawhorses, and slide inside her heat. But it wasn't just about getting his dick wet. It was a need to touch her, to make her come, to make her *his*.

And when she came to him wanting sex, he wanted it to be because she wanted him, not out of some need to keep herself safe from the others. Was that too much to ask?

Maybe, but he couldn't help it.

VISIT HTTPS://LIZASTREETAUTHOR.COM/FILTHY-ALPHA to get your copy of *Filthy Alpha*!

ALSO BY LIZA STREET

Fierce Mates: Dark Pines Pride

Wild Homecoming

Wild Atonement

Wild Reunion

Wild Engagement

∾

Fierce Mates: Rock Creek Clan

The Rose King

Ruthless Misfit

Ruthless Outlaw

Ruthless Fighter

Ruthless Rogue

Ruthless Knight

∾

Junkyard Shifters

Filthy Vandal

Filthy Beast

Filthy Wolf

Filthy Alpha

∾

Spellbound Shifters: Dragons Entwined

(with Keira Blackwood)

Dragon Forgotten (a FREE prequel)

Dragon Shattered

Dragon Unbroken

Dragon Reborn

Dragon Ever After

Spellbound Shifters: Fates and Visions

(with Keira Blackwood)

Oracle Defiant

Oracle Adored

Spellcaster Hidden

Spellbound Shifters Standalones

(with Keira Blackwood)

Hope Reclaimed

Orphan Entangled

Alphas & Alchemy: Fierce Mates

(with Keira Blackwood)

Claimed in Forbidden

Fated in Forbidden

Bound to Forbidden

Caught in Forbidden

Mated in Forbidden

Forever in Forbidden

ABOUT LIZA

Liza likes her heroes packing muscles and her heroines packing agency. She got her start in romance by sneak-reading her grandma's paperbacks. Now she's a *USA Today* bestselling author and she spends her time writing about hot shifters with fierce and savage hearts.

Join Liza's mailing list to get all the good news when it happens! Visit https://lizastreetauthor.com/free-book/